ORDER
OF THE
VOID

ROBERT VAUGHN

Edited by: Floyd Largent

Cover Art By: Mr. Wolf

Copyright © 2020 by Robert J. Vaughn.

The following is a work of fiction. Any and all names, characters, places and events are the creation of the author. Any and all resemblance to persons, living or dead and purely coincidental. This is a work of fiction meant to be enjoyed.

Print ISBN: 978-0-578-69737-6

Ebook ISBN: 978-0-578-69738-3

Other Works

Chapter 1

Rain drizzles over the gravesite, as it has all day; it seems appropriate for the occasion. As the funeral services end, I somberly make my way to the closed casket and place my hand on the top. I look at the casket, still shocked that a friend of mine is dead; and finally I manage to choke out, "This isn't 'goodbye,' Bret. This is 'I'll see you later'."

I trudge over to Bret's mother and say in a low voice, "Bret was a great person, Ms. Pearsmith," then hug her.

Tissues still in hand, Mrs. Pearsmith wipes her eyes. Honestly, I can't tell if it's the rain, tears, or both she's wiping away. "Thank you, Jeffery," she replies in a weary, breathy voice. "He always had nothing but good things to say about you."

"Thank you. We were good friends. If you need anything, let me know, okay? I mean it. You have my number."

She smiles and nods. "I appreciate that, but I'm going to Canada for a while. To spend time with family. I just need to get away, you know?"

"Yeah, I understand. I'd do the same thing."

She nods again. "Can you follow me to the limo? Bret wanted me to give you something."

"Yes, ma'am, of course."

As we walk to the limo, I wondered what Bret's left me. Once there, she asks the driver to open up the trunk. When he does, Ms. Pearsmith removes a shoebox and hands to me. "He sent this to me with a note, saying to give this you. I don't know what's inside. I figured it's something personal between the two of you."

I look at the box, confused. "Um thank you. I don't know what's in it either." I turn my attention back to her. "I'm sorry if this is the wrong time to ask, but did the police give you any new information about what happened?"

She shakes her head and sighs. "No, all I know is what they already told me. They found him tied up, with a gunshot wound to his head. Was Bret into anything strange at all?"

"Not that I know of. The last time I talked to him was two days before he died, and he seemed fine." I sigh, looking at her. "I wish I had more information for you, ma'am."

"I know, Jeffery. If anything comes up, I'll let you know. I promise."

"I'll do the same for you." I thank her, and we hug one last time before we part ways.

I don't know it at the time, but I've lied to her. As it turns out, the truth is too painful and horrific for her to ever know.

Later, back at my apartment, I sit down at my computer desk and open up the shoebox to see what's inside. I find some pictures of a couple I don't recognize, some defaced; a used black candle; and a thumb drive. As I paw through the box to see if anything else is in there, I get an email notification on my cell phone; my eyes go wide in shock when I see that it's from Bret's email address. Confused, at first I figure this is some sick joke, but I open the email anyway. All I see is a video file attachment. I run the file through a virus scan before I open it, and it comes back clean.

When I open the file, I'm shocked to see Bret on my screen, sitting in front of the camera in his living room, looking gloriously alive. "Hey, Jeffery. I'm gonna cut straight to the point: I'm dead. The only way you'll ever see this video is if you receive it through what I call a deadman drop. If I don't reply to an automated system

every three days, then it automatically emails this video to you.

"I... I accidentally got involved in something dangerous."

After taking a deep breath, he continues, "Okay. All this started

when I ordered one of those deep-web mystery boxes just for kicks. I

figured I would get on the bandwagon of making an unboxing video

and make a quick buck or two. I didn't get what I expected. I did

some digging to find out more about the stuff in the box. It's all

linked to a friggin' cult, and I know this cult is coming after me now.

Every time I've tried to upload a video about the cult, it's been taken

down in the blink of an eye. I was told time and again by the admins

of site after site that the reason was because it broke the terms of

service. Soon all my accounts got taken down, and I couldn't create

new ones. I didn't want to tell you this sooner for your safety, but I

know they won't stop until someone stops them — or at the very

least, until the general public knows about them." His eyes flick to

the right, and the next words come in a rush: "You have a large

Internet following that you can use to spread the word about this

cult. I'm snail-mailing my mom everything that was in the mystery box to give to you when I die, okay? And I know I'm gonna die. It's inevitable. So I need your help from beyond the grave. Please bring this cult down and stop them.

"Thanks, Jeffery. You've been a great friend, and I... I'll miss you." The video cuts out.

Chapter 2

That's a helluva thing to dump on someone, good friend or not.

I pace around living room, muttering. "What the hell did you *do*, Bret? Why the hell would some cult come after you?" I stop pacing and stand there, just looking at the stuff from the shoebox. "You sent this to me because you think I can, I don't know, save the day? Okay, Bret, this was your dying wish. But if I die, I'm kicking your ass in the afterlife."

An idea comes to mind on how to get the ball rolling. I wrap the shoebox up in brown packing paper that I have lying around from a package I got earlier, address it to myself to make it seem like I just got this delivered, and set things up for a new vlog entry.

❖

"What's up, guys? It's your boy, Jeffery B. Before we get started, please follow me on all social media — Instagram, Facebook, JustDoIt, Twitter, and et cetera! Crush that Like button, ya'll. Because by you guys supporting me, we can make this community grow and reach that goal of one meeelllion followers!" I do my best Dr. Evil impression, pinky to the corner of my lips, then clap my hands together and smile widely.

"So: I saw all those videos about people ordering these deep-web mystery boxes and I thought, whassup with that? So I figured I would see what the big deal is."

I point at the shoebox with both my index fingers in excitement. "We have it here, and we are about to get into it and see what's inside! Like always in life, safety is critical. So, I will put my medical gloves on that I got from the pharmacy down the street. Pristine purple nitrile, yo." I grab the box of gloves, pull two out, and put them on with great fanfare. I figure this will hype things up. Next, I grab a pocketknife and cut just enough of the packing tape off so I'm able to grab the items inside the box. "Okay, we're in! Let's look inside and see what a hundred bucks got us."

Peeling away the tape, I continue, "Now, before you guys start saying I'm dumb for doing this, don't worry. I used a P.O. box, not my actual address." Once the tape is off, I open the box and start to take the items out and hold them up to the camera for people to see. "Okay, not as much as I expected. We have a plastic sandwich bag with some pictures in it. A skinny black candle that's already been used, and, oh-ho, a regular thumb drive! Is it full of porn? A saucy novel? Someone's video diary? A copy of *The Ring*? Weeeelll, I'll save what's on the thumb drive for last. If it's anything gory or too porny or something that, it would get me in trouble with the site, so I'm going to censor it if I have to and just describe it to you guys."

I stare at the thumb drive, wondering what's on there, seeing as how I haven't checked it out myself yet.

I reach over to the bag with the pictures. "I will cut the camera off first and just spread them out, then move the camera around so you can see them all. So that's why there'll be the jump cut." The camera cuts off as promised, then turns back on with a wide shot looking down at the photos. There are six: three rows of two each. "All righty then. Here are the photos... and now things are getting creepy. We have three copies of a picture of a man, smiling for the camera in the first picture. The second picture has black candle wax all over the man's face, most likely the wax from the very candle we looked at earlier. The last photo of the man has his face cut out of it. Creepy. Now. The other three pictures are three copies a lady. Like the guy in the first picture, everything looks normal. The second one has wax on it, and the third one has her face cut out. I don't know who these people are. Never seen 'en before. I'll scan the clean pictures into my computer and do an image search and see what happens. Here's where I clean up the photos and get everything set up to look at what's on the thumb drive, so I'll cut it here. My next video will be me looking at the thumb drive and what's on it. In the comments for this viddy, tell me what you think is on the video. Follow me on social media and on this site, and leave comments. Love you guys, and I'll see you next video."

I cut the video off and just sit there. "Did you know these people, Bret?" I ask no one in particular.

Chapter 3

I double-check everything to make sure everything it's good to go before I start recording. I set it up for picture-in-picture. The video on the thumb drive will play on the larger screen, while my face will be on the smaller one. Once everything is ready, I start it up.

"Okay, peeps, Jeffery B. here, back in black, to quote AC/DC! Before we get started, remember to follow me here and on all my social media. Like always, speak your mind in the Comments section down below." I point downward.

"I read your comments for the last video, like always, and I know you're hungry for more. I wanted you guys to share what you think is on the thumb drive. Some of you said it would be some fake, edgy art video. Someone of you said it's the movie of a serial killer killing someone and recording it for everyone to see. Brrr. Me personally, I have no idea what it could be. I still haven't looked. Before I even plugged it in, I disconnected my computer from the Internet. I don't know what's on here, so better safe than sorry, right?

If it has anything crazy on it like murder or gore or creepy stuff to do with kids, I *will* censor it, and if I can, I'll describe it to you."

I'm feeling a mixture of all kinds of emotions as I prepare to view the contents of the drive. Mostly fear, because whatever was on this thumb drive most likely got Bret killed. On the outside, though, I have to play it calm, cool, and collected. I have to get it out there to help avenge my friend, no matter what it is. So I point both my index fingers at myself. "I'm ready!" I look at the camera. "You better be ready. Let's dive in and see what's up. First, I'll run a standard virus scan." I click over to the virus scan program I already have open and let the program do its thing. It quickly finishes, showing that there are only three files are on the drive, and that there is no viruses, worms, malware, or anything else that can damage my computer accompanying them. I suddenly wish that it could detect evil magic, but quash that silly thought.

I highlight the thumb drive directory, so all my viewers can see it. "Okay, so that's the thumb drive. It's just named Book 1." I double-click. "Okay, so there are three files. Looks like two pictures and a movie file. One picture file is named 'Carmen Fairfield,' and the other is 'Reginald Fairfield'. Brother and sister? Husband and wife? Let's see if we can get a clue or two."

I double-click on both of the pictures so they open. The one titled "Reginald Fairfield" is a picture of a black man. He looks to be in his mid-30s, and is clean-shaven. The file named "Carmen" is a picture of a white woman. She has long, straight black hair, and also looks in her mid-30s as well. I know neither of them. "Okay, we have two people. Same last name. I think they're husband and wife. No idea who these people are."

Nervous and yet excited, it hits me like a ton of bricks. "Hey, wait! Holy shit, guys, those are the same people from the photos in the last video!" I hit my Drama Button, and the "Duh DUHHHHH!" echoes over the video.

"Okay, folks, time to play the movie file. Like I said, if it's something like gore, kids, or anything else that would warrant me getting kicked off the site, I will censor it so you can't see it, and if I can, I will explain to you what I see." I double-click on the file to open it. When the video first opens, I know within seconds that it will have to be censored. My body rears back in surprise at what I see and hear.

"Whoa! Okay, guys, this going to be censored for sure!" I move in closer to get a better look. I make an audible gulp, and my eyes go wide. All that the audience will see is a blur, but they will hear a man and woman whimpering. "Holy shit, holy shit, holy shit." I immediately pause the video and look at the camera with my eyes wide, at a complete loss for words. I take a deep breath to regain some composure, so I can explain what I saw. "Okay, people, so I see Reginald and Carmen, the people from the photo. They're, um, they're on their knees naked, with their hands and feet tied behind them. Their mouths are gagged with what I guess are bondage ball-gags. Not really my scene. The lighting is pretty low, and it looks like they're in some old run-down room. Maybe in the back of a warehouse. They're bleeding from all over their bodies. I don't know what caused the bleeding or why. I may have to take this to the police if it's more than just, you know, BDSM stuff."

Feeling a little sick, I wonder silently, *Is this what happened to you, Bret?*

After taking a deep breath, I press play and turn my attention back to the video. I see a person in an emerald-green hooded robe holding a black candle in both hands step into the frame. The candle is lit, dribbling hot wax on their hands; the person's face is hidden behind a cheap green Halloween mask. They intone in an androgynous voice, "Praise be to Rojachar. For Rojachar is The Great Void. For Rojachar is The Great Devourer. Everything that Rojachar devourers is baptized in his blood and reborn anew! Praise be to Rojachar!" Off camera, I can hear other voices saying, "Praise Rojachar."

"Tonight, we baptize these two," says the robed figure. They then pour hot, black candle wax on the two victims. As the wax hits their bodies, their muffled whimpering and cries of pain become even more audible. "Their blood mixes with the blood of Rojachar, baptizing them and making them one with Rojachar!" the hooded figure exults.

Fuck, this is weird. Is this some kind of college prank? Some kind of sex orgy cult?

I pause the video and look at the camera, and I can see that my face is pale, with spots of color high on my cheeks like they've been rouged. "Okay. We have some person in a green cloak with a hood over his or her head and a green mask covering his or her face. As this person is speaking about this Rojachar person or thing, he's pouring black candle wax on Reginald's and Carmen's heads and all over their bodies. From the sounds they're making, it's pretty painful. Other voices are talking, but are out of frame." I un-pause the video.

The cloaked figure, whom I think of as the high priest, hands the black candle to a person out of frame, and in return, they give him a knife. A fucking knife! "Now that we have baptized them, they will leave this world and go into the next!" he exclaims. "Their souls will be feasted upon by Rojachar, and become one with him. Their souls will fuel The Great Void! The Great Devourer! Praise be to Rojachar!"

After his demonic sermon, Reginald and Carmen struggle vigorously to get free. As they do so, muffled cries and yells of terror escape their mouths. I have my hands over my own mouth in shock. I breathe deeper and quicker, and my heart races faster and faster as the video continues. Four other people, also in green

hooded robes and masks, rush into the frame and grab the terrified

couple, pinning them down to the ground on their backs.

The cloaked figure with the knife kneels, and looks at the

couple before speaking to them in a calm, nurturing voice, as if the

two were his children. "I release you to Rojachar, Carmen and

Reginald. I envy you, for the next time you wake up, you will know

bliss." With that said, he takes a deep breath and turns his attention

to the man. At breakneck speed, he stabs Reginald with the knife,

repeatedly, all over his upper body, starting at his belly and working

his way up to his neck. He repeats the same up and down pattern one

more time, then turns to Carmen and does the same to her. I see so

much blood gush from their bodies and splatter over the four

accomplices and the killer himself that I can't help but lean over and

puke into my trash can.

I straighten up, wiping my mouth. I'm completely shocked, at

a loss for words and visibly shaken up. The one thing that is seared

into my head is their eyes. I saw the life in their eyes fade away with each gasping breath. As the breathing stopped, they laid there on the ground lifeless, but still had that terrified look in their eyes.

Their lifeless expressions are asking, "Why us? We're good people and try to do right!"

The movie ends with a close-up of their faces.

My hands are still over my mouth in shock. My eyes quickly dart back and forth from the camera to my computer screen. My eyes are filled with horror. I have no idea what to say, do, or even think. I take my hands away from my mouth and look again. This looks terribly real, and I'm convinced I just witnessed a murder. I finally croak to my audience, "What I just s-saw was the, the cloaked guy... stabbing the couple. To death. Guys, these weren't a few stabs; he must have stabbed them a dozen times each. Blood was everywhere. It looked entirely real. This was fucking brutal — that's the only way I can explain it. I don't know what to do. I don't know if I should even post this. Should I just throw everything away? Should I tell the police? Am I going to get in trouble if I tell them? That was just... holy *shit*." I reach over off and turn the camera off, trembling

"Did something like that happen to you, Bret?" I ask my dear departed friend. As usual, he doesn't answer.

Chapter 4

I post the video after blurring out the images of the victims and re-engaging the Internet. I don't even edit out me puking. I ask my followers what I should do next. I've already decided to go to the police.

I get back to my followers the next week, live this time. All my normal enthusiasm and bonhomie are gone. "Hey everyone, Jeffery B. here. No gimmicks or anything like that today. This video will go over the awful things that happened in the last video. To make a long, nasty story short, I ordered a mystery box off the deep web. It had some crazy stuff in it, but most important was what was on the thumb drive. First there were two pictures. One was of a man, Reginald, and the other was of a woman, his wife Carmen. Also on the drive was a video of what I'm guessing is a cult killing Reginald and Carmen for someone or something named Rojachar. After watching that, I was pretty shaken up, and just needed to step away from my social media to process all that, and figure out what to do. I read your posts, and most of you said to go to the police. I did that. I took the box to the police station and told them everything that happened. They told me I'm not in any trouble, but that said they would get in contact with me if they have any more questions. The next day a detective got in touch with me. I told the detective everything that happened. He's seen the video, too. He's investigating it. So now, I sit back and wait."

I sigh heavily and bury my face in my hands, trying to think of what to say next, wondering what Bret had to do with all of this. I look up back at the camera, my face haggard. "I did a bit of digging to kill my curiosity. I looked around on the Internet to see if I could find any news articles, any missing persons reports, or whether any creators on the site who are big into the true crime stuff did a video on the Fairfields or Rojachar. I was able to find a few things."

The video cuts away from me, and on screen are two missing persons flyers picturing the Fairfields. "Reginald and Carmen Fairfield were last seen on May 17, 2017. They were from Houston, Texas. They were both last seen at a bar named Danny's Pub and Grub. I live here in Houston and have been to Danny's before. It's in a nice part of town, the stereotypical suburbs. Pretty plain, and not much happens there. It's not like downtown, with all the clubs and stuff.

"Reginald was a project manager for an company called Foresight Oil and Gas." The video cuts to the company logo. "Carmen was a fourth-grade teacher at a school called Edward Herman Elementary." The video cuts to a very nice-looking school. "Friends and family told the police that there were no problems in their relationship. They said the Fairfields were head-over-heels for one another. They were your everyday couple, except maybe a little happier."

The video cuts away from the school and then to a selfie of the happy couple hanging out at Danny's with some friends. "This is the last image of them out in public. Friends said that it was typical night. Neither had much to drink. Reginald had a beer and some food. Carmen had a glass of wine, and she didn't even finish it. She also had some food as well. So they weren't drunk, and it's unlikely that someone drugged them. The Fairfields left at about 9:30 that night. Friends said it was a good night.

"The next day, neither of them showed up for work. They didn't call in or anything like that. Reginald's mother was contacted by his job because she was marked as one of his emergency contacts. They tried calling his wife first, but she didn't pick up. The mom called the police to do a welfare check to see what was going on. Police went to the Fairfields' home, and here's the odd part. Both cars were still there, and there were no signs of a break in. Both their phones were in Reginald's car, along with the keys. Police went inside the house, and everything was fine. Nothing stolen. It's as if these two just disappeared into thin air. Police questioned family, friends, and coworkers. No one raised any alarms to the police, so the police had no evidence to go on. Zero suspects, zero clues, nothing at all. Fast forward to now. That's when we see the Fairfields on the video. Problem is, we don't know when the video was made. It could have been made the day of their disappearance, it could have been last month; I don't know. Hopefully, now that I've turned everything over to the police, that will help them track down their killers — and at the very least, give their families some closure."

I shrug and throw my hands up in defeat. "That's all I have for now, guys. I've done everything I can with this. Next week, if I'm up to it, we'll get back to our regularly scheduled program of deep-web exploring. Also, some new video games came out, so I may review those. A lot of you guys have also asked me about live-streaming some deep-web browsing. Let me think about that one, and I'll see what's up. I'm not sure I want to do that after this debacle. Anyway, that's all I have today. Stay awesome, and I'll see you guys next time."

I turn the camera off, and just sit there, going over what's been happening over the past week. "Were you part of the cult, Bret? I hope not." I shake my head firmly. "No. Can't be. It's not like you. Even if you joined, why *would* you?"

Chapter 5

The video turns on, and this time I'm sitting inside a hotel room. Usually, I'm a one-man show, but this time is different. "What's up, guys? It's me, Jeffery B. No new deep-web browsing or game reviews today, sorry. The mystery continues with the Fairfields. If you need to be caught up, I have links down below of videos that will do just that. If you're not caught up, press pause, go watch the videos, come back, and press play."

I wait a moment before I continue. "Okay, so I'm here in East Texas in the town of Fur Grove, with someone I will refer to as David. That's not his real name, so don't bother looking for him. He's not even from Fur Grove, okay? He saw my vlogs and contacted me. He wants to have his face blurred and voice altered to have his identity protected. He has some info regarding the whole Rojachar cult. So, I'm just going to let him talk and share what he knows."

"Thank you for having me," 'David' says, sounding like Darth Vader, his face pixilated beyond recognition. "I'm a big fan of true crime vlogs and stuff like. When you started talking about this cult, it got me thinking about a case I was following.

"This cult has been around for years." David takes out a folder and opens it. He removes out a police report from 2012. "This is a case about a 23-year-old freshman named Shawn Buckmen. Shawn was your typical college freshman. He came from a good family and had a lot of good friends."

"Mind if make a copy this to add to my stuff that I've found out about this cult?" I asked him.

David nods and hands it to me. "Take it. I have copies of everything, and the police redacted anything important, like the names of the cops involved."

"What makes Shawn so important?" I ask.

"Nothing — that's the crazy part. Shawn and his friends went to a house party that was being held at a mutual friend's place. Friends said that everything went fine. It was your everyday college party. Shawn and his friends had too much to drink, so they all crashed at this friend's place. Next morning everyone wakes up to get some breakfast. Problem is, Shawn is... " David takes out a missing person flyer with a picture of Shawn on it. "Shawn is nowhere to found."

I shrug, thinking there had to be a good reason Shawn wasn't there with everyone else. "Maybe he sobered up and walked back to his dorm?"

David nods. "That's what everyone thought. They tried calling him, but there was no answer. So they figured he was sleeping off a hangover, and they'd catch up with him later. After breakfast, they called him again, and there's still no answer. Now his friends were worried. They went by his dorm, and his roommate said he hadn't seen him since he left for the party. Police got involved, and they looked for him.

"Here's where things get crazy. Six days later, police tell the public they've found Shawn in a ditch somewhere. Police said he was killed during a mugging."

I look at him, confused. "What's crazy about that?"

"I'll show you. Don't ask me how I got this; I keep my sources private." David pulls out a picture I know I will have to censor. He points to the picture. "That's Shawn right here. They actually found him in a rundown cabin, naked, stab wounds all over him, covered in black candle wax." David pulls out a few sheets of paper. "This is the police report discussing how they found the body." He places a few more papers on the desk. "This is autopsy report. Cause of death was multiple stab wounds.

"Now, this is a town of about 33,000, and most of the people are students of McCraney University. The police had never seen anything like this. They don't know how to handle it. My source told me they called the FBI. Feds come to town, and they show them this." He takes out four more pictures; they will need to be censored as well. "Debbie Finton died in 2001. Clint Peterson died in 1999. Paige Johnson died in 1995. Melvin Martinez died in 1990. All from different walks of life. All different ages. All different races. Both sexes. All died of stab wounds, and were found with black candle wax on their bodies. Feds tell the local police to tell the public that Shawn was killed in a robbery gone wrong."

"That makes no sense. If you have a cult going around killing people, why keep it out of the public eye?" I ask David.

"Think about it. One serial killer is enough. You tell the public you have a *group* of serial killers working together, a group working as a hive mind made up of twisted individuals AND they haven't been caught yet, and people would lose their shit." David packs all the files into the folder and slides it over to me. "Let me ask you something. Why are you researching this crazy killer cult?"

I don't want to tell him or anyone else why I'm doing this. Maybe I want to keep it private. Maybe I just don't trust anyone else with my reasons. If Bret wanted to people to know about it, they would have known. "I didn't think it would get this far," I lie. "I just ordered a deep-web mystery box. I didn't know it would turn into something like this. Plus, if there's some serial killer group out there, the public has a right to know."

"I'm not trying to tell you what to do, man. But my advice to you is to stop what you're doing. Don't let Internet fame get you in trouble or killed," David says.

That's where I end the video.

❖

A few hours go by, and now I'm alone in my hotel room. I sat in front of my laptop camera in my hotel room. No need to edit this video. I just want to talk to the fans one on one.

"Hey, guys, I'm here in the hotel room still. David's gone. I should sleep, but I can't. I'm thinking about everything that's been going on.

"After talking with David, I needed to get my mind off everything, recharge, and look at everything with a clear head. So I gamed, had some dinner, and took a shower. After my shower, I sat down and looked at everything again. Honestly, I have nothing new. I mean, I don't know what to make of this. This started out as just a video to jump on the bandwagon of these deep-web mystery boxes, most of which are fake, by the way. I didn't think this would lead to a serial killer cult." I shake my head and shrug, not having an idea of what to do next. "Anyways, guys, I'm going to try and get some sleep. I'll see you next time."

Chapter 6

It's been a week since I posted a video. Aside from a short catnap here and there, it's been almost three days since I've slept. I've been going through my videos and the stuff that David gave me, thinking maybe I missed something. Going through the video that Bret sent me. Thinking that maybe there's that one clue that detectives in movies always find, the one that cracks the case wide open. I didn't have that luck.

A few hours pass, and I take a break. Bret said that he ordered the package off the deep web. I look through the sea of dead websites, hitmen-for-hire sites, drugs for sale websites, counterfeit cash stores, and other oddities one finds on the deep web. Eventually, I come across a video-sharing site. I look around to find anything worthwhile, trying various key words. One video catches my attention: the title is "Praise The Great Void." As I watch the video, my eyes go wide.

Once the video finishes, I'm once again at a loss for words. I get out my camera and make sure everything else is good to go before I started recording a new vlog entry. Once everything is ready, I pressed Record on the camera.

On the screen is the home page of a website called WeScreen. On the bottom left side of the screen is a smaller window with my face. "Sorry if I look haggard," I tell my viewers. "I haven't been getting much sleep lately. I've been going through everything I have. That's why there's been the social media silence. I didn't find anything that stood out. So I decided to look through deep web, thinking I'd find some new info.

"And I did. I just found this website called WeScreen. It's set up like any other video-sharing site you would find on the surface web." I click on another tab, and now on the screen is the video I saw earlier, only this time blurred out for anyone who might watch my vlog. "While looking around, I found this video called 'Praise The Great Void.' Just a heads-up, everyone, this will be censored, and you'll soon understand why."

I press play. On my screen, not the one that the audience can see, is a naked young woman. Blood covers most of her body, oozing from fresh cuts. The young 20-something looks like she could be a prom queen. She sits there on her knees with her hands resting on her thighs. Unlike the Fairfields, she lacks a look of terror. Instead, she bears a look of pride on her face, all while being surrounded by people in black cloaks and black masks that cover their faces — with a single individual in an emerald-green cloak with an emerald-green mask overseeing it all.

I pause the video and look at the camera. "Okay, so we have the fucking cult again, and there's a girl who looks to be in her early 20s covered in blood and cuts. The odd thing is that she's not acting scared at all. She's sitting proudly, ready for what's next." I press play to start the video back up.

The figure in the green cloak walks over to the bloody woman and stands in front of her. "Don't worry; soon you will be one with Rojachar." This time the cloaked person's voice is female.

The naked girl nods. "Yes, I am ready to become one with The Great Void."

The green figure turns away from the girl and faces the others in the room. "Hail Rojachar! Praise to the Great Void!" The others, along with the naked woman, echo the emerald-cloaked figure in the same passionate tone.

"Tonight, Kimberly Ann Thompson is becoming one with the void. She will give strength to Rojachar so that he may perform The Great Unification! She, like those before her, has taken it upon herself to achieve the ultimate accomplishment in their lives! That accomplishment is to be baptized!" the cloaked woman preaches as she and the other cloaked figures are seen clapping and cheering for Kimberly.

The figure walks around and stands behind Kimberly, then places her hands on her shoulders. Once behind her, everyone stops cheering and goes silent. "Are you ready, Kimberly Ann Thompson?" When asked, the girl nods, not saying anything. The green-cloaked figure reaches off the frame and returns with a black lit candle. She pours the candle wax on the crown of Kimberly's head and then over the rest of her body, most notably on the cuts. "Tonight, Kimberly Ann Thompson, your blood mixes with his blood. You will be one with him." As the candle wax drips on her body, she winces in pain slightly, but she is still sitting proudly.

The leader blows out the candle and hands it to someone off the frame, then comes back on frame with a knife. The cloaked figure raises the knife in the air, holding it with both hands tightly, looking up at it. "Tonight, I release you from this world! Go and be one with Rojachar!" That said, the cloaked figure violently stabs Kimberly, each stab just as vicious as the last. As Kimberly is being stabbed, there is no look of fear or pain on her face; her expression is blissful.

Unable to watch anymore, I quickly close all the windows on screen and look at the camera. Wanting to end this quickly, I blurt, "Okay, so like the Fairfields, the woman had wax poured on her body. She then gets stabbed, but she doesn't have a look of pain; she looks happy. That's fucked up." I'm speaking in a panicked voice. "And yeah, that's it for now. I'll talk to you guys later. " I quickly turn the camera off and bend over at the waist, hugging myself, trying not to puke.

Chapter 7

It's 11 AM the next day. I tried to get a full night of sleep last night, but I wasn't able to. That last video was seared into my brain, replaying repeatedly. I sit there at my desk, drinking my coffee, thinking. I have a name. Kimberly Ann Thompson. My best bet would be to track down someone who knew her.

After digging around on social media, it doesn't take me long to find her sister. She works for a marketing firm in Phoenix, Arizona. I find her work email and contact her. In the email, I explain who I am, and what I'm doing. I tell her I saw a video of her sister online. We email back forth, and I tell her where she can find the video. I ask her if she will agree to a video call, and if I can record it. About 30 minutes go by before I got a reply from her saying she can talk in an hour, and she leaves me her contact info so I can video-call her.

An hour goes by, and I call her. She answers, her face grim. I say, "Hey, Shelly, thank you for taking the time to talk. I just want to let you know once more, before we keep going, that I'll record this. I want people out there to know that there's a serial killer cult out there, and that the police are covering this up."

Shelly takes a deep breath and nods. "Yes, I understand. Anything to get my sister's story out there so this doesn't happen to anyone else."

"Thank you very much." I mess around on my computer to make sure everything is good to go. "Shelly, please introduce yourself, and just go from there."

"Hello, everyone, my name is Shelly Maria Thompson. Kimberly was my older sister. I'm 22, and my sister was 25 when she died a year ago. The police told my family it was a botched robbery. Then Jeffery contacted me and he told me what really happened." She takes a deep breath, trying to hold back her tears. She grabs a nearby tissue and wipes her eyes, sniffling a bit "I don't think I'll tell my family what really happened. They're just now slowly starting to come to terms with everything. I think it's for the best."

She sobs a minute before she regains her composure. She the smiles brightly at the camera before speaking again. "Kimberly was just awesome. We were total opposites. Honestly, I think that's why we got along so well. The whole opposites attract thing." Shelly laughs a bit. "I was the tomboy of the two, always getting trouble. Kimberly was prom queen and a captain of the cheerleading squad. She didn't let the popularity go to her head. She hung out with everyone. Her best friend in high school, Stacy, was part of the goth clique.

"Kimberly and Stacy were still hanging out before she died. Stacy took it hard. The depression won, and she took her own life. Her husband found her dead next to an empty bottle of sleeping pills and vodka." She wipes her eyes.

"I'm sorry for the loss of your sister and her best friend. Kimberly sounded like she was a great person," I tell her in a soothing tone, trying to make her feel better.

Shelly nods sharply. "Thank you very much. Like I said, Kimberly was awesome." She laughs after saying that, most likely thinking about the good times she had with her sister.

"You told me she was missing for a week before they found her body. What can you tell me about the final days you spent with her?" I ask Shelley.

"They were normal. Kimberly reached 1 million followers on her makeup review vlog. She was an influencer. She was getting paid for it, too, so career-wise she was doing great. She didn't have any relationship problems, because she was too busy with her vlog to have a boyfriend. She was focused on her vlog. Although her very last vlog was strange."

"Strange how?" I ask.

"It started with her reviewing some lipstick by her favorite makeup company. After the makeup review, though, she started talking about how that would be her last vlog, and that she was going away."

"Was she under some stress? Maybe a fan turned stalker?"

Shelly shakes her head. "No stress, as far as I know. If she was under stress, she hid it well. As for her fans, she had no problems with her fans throughout her years of vlogging." A tear runs down her face, and she wipes it away. "I didn't really follow her content. I'm not big into makeup, so didn't see that video till after she went missing. The last time I saw her was in the afternoon the day before she went missing. We had lunch, and everything was fine."

"What happened next?" I ask her.

"Sunday I was out running errands, and I wasn't far from Kimberly's place, so I decided to stop by and surprise her. I started knocking on the door. I figured she was home, because her car was in the parking lot. I got my cell phone out and called her so she could come to the door and answer it. Then I took out my copy of the key to her apartment to let myself in, but noticed that the door was already unlocked. Something didn't feel right, so I called the cops. They searched her place, and there was no sign of a break-in or any foul play. My family and I filed a missing persons report. The community helped us out, but unfortunately, we found nothing." She can't hold it together, and starts crying.

Concerned for her wellbeing, I chime in, "We can stop if you want."

She shakes her head. "No, I can keep going." She grabs some tissues and wipes her face. "A week later, the police found her body out in the woods, with multiple stab wounds." Her sorrowful look turns into a look of confusion. "I don't understand why the cops told us one thing, but something different happened."

"Did the cops tell you anything different than they told the public?" I ask.

She wipes her eyes and blows her nose. "No, nothing. Everything I know the public know, but there was something odd at the station."

"Define odd."

"While the local cops were doing what they needed to do, there were these two men in suits hanging around... I just figured they were FBI or something, and shrugged it off. The whole time they were there, they directed traffic. I thought nothing of it, but after what you told me, it makes sense that they were there."

"Is there anything else you can think of? Maybe anything else you may have left out?" I prompt, hoping she has more for me to go on.

She shook her head in response. "No, nothing. I just want to say thank you for getting Kimberly's real story out there."

"No, thank you, Shelly. This info is a lot of help. I'm so sorry for your loss." We say our goodbyes, and the call ends.

❖

It's the day after I posted the interview with Shelly. I fell asleep at my desk, looking over the information I had collected so far, but the sound of my doorbell and phone ringing wake me and alert me that someone is at the door . It takes a few seconds for my mind to catch up with my body as I grab my phone and open up the app that allows me to see who's at the door via the camera on the doorbell. On cam are a man and a woman in black suits. I tap on the screen so we can speak through the intercom on the doorbell. "Can I help you?" I ask in a groggy tone.

"Hello, I'm Special Agent Miller," says the man. He points to the woman next to him. "This is Special Agent Hayes." They take out their badges and hold them to the camera so I can see. "We're with the government, and we want to talk to you about your vlog."

I look at the badges. From my viewpoint, they look like official police badges, but instead of saying something like "FBI" they read "United States Special Security."

I raised an eyebrow and question them. "I've never heard of Special Security."

"I assure you, we are with the government," the woman responds.

"Sure, okay, and I'm the Queen of England." I reply sarcastically.

They put their badges way, and the male agent pulls his cell phone from his jacket pocket and starts flipping through it. "Jeffery Alexander Bailey. Born March 23, 1996. Currently 23 years old. Son of Jill Alexander and Patrick Bailey. Went by 'Xander' in grade school until a bully beat it out of you." He goes into details about things I never shared on the vlog before. He mentions the elementary school and high school I went to. My Social Security Number. My social media habits. My first sexual experience. Even my credit score.

My heart races in panic as he continues to recite my personal information. Maybe they're here to shut me up. I shake my head, thinking they can't be here for that. People have posted much worse on the site than me. I decide I have to answer the door. I really don't have a choice, do I?

"Ummm yeah, hang on. I just woke up." I get up from my desk and stare at the door, taking a few deep breaths before walking to it. From my desk to the door takes just a few seconds, but my nervousness makes it seem like forever. I grasp the doorknob and take another deep breath before unlocking the door and cracking it open just slightly. "Morning. How can I help you?"

The agent puts his phone back into the inner breast pocket of his suit jacket. "We just want to talk to you about a few things. Mind if my partner and I come in?" Miller asks in tone that suggests we've been friends for years.

"Yeah. I, I mean, we mind." I blurt.

"We?" the female agent asks.

I nod at them. "Yeah, my girlfriend is here, and she's not a huge fan of law enforcement. Am I in trouble or something?" I ask, trying to sound convincing.

They both look at each other, then back at me. "We also know that you're single. Now may we come in?" the female agent asks forcefully.

I shake my head. "No, you can't come in. Look, what's this about? It's not a crime to vlog about stuff. I did what was right, and everything was in the box I gave to the cops. I don't know how to find David. Shouldn't you guys be tracking down the real criminals? Anyway, how did you guys find me?!" I protest, raising my voice, more nervous than anything else, trying to make a scene in hopes my neighbors will come out to see what's going.

The female agent smirks. "We're the government, Mr. Bailey. You're also correct. Legally, you have not committed a crime. But for your own safety, stop the vlogs," she tells me in a slightly concerning voice.

Miller hands me a card with his contact info. "If you ever need to talk," he says neutrally. The two agents turn and walk down the hallway. I go back inside my apartment and quickly lock the door, then sit down on my couch and take a few deep breaths to calm myself. It takes me a while, but I'm finally able to calm down. I open the app on my phone to look through the camera on the doorbell to

make sure they aren't outside. I sigh in relief upon not seeing them.

Chapter 8

An hour has gone by since the government agents paid me a visit. I pick up the card from my desk and look closely at it. I sit down and open up a search engine on the deep web, and type in "United States Special Security." Nothing worthwhile pops up. I type in the phone number, and nothing comes up. Try their names and nothing comes up. There's no address on the card, so I can't search that. I sit there looking at the keyboard, tapping my fingers against it, trying to figure out what to do next. *Did these same people visit Bret?* I wonder.

I decide to do a live-stream of me gaming. I need to give my mind a break and focus on something fun. I make a post on my social media, saying I'll stream in thirty minutes. That should give me enough time to make a quick bite to eat.

❖

Thirty minutes have come and gone. I sit down at my desk, put my headset on, and start everything up. "What's up, guys, it's

Jeffery B. Welcome to the live stream. Before we get things started, make sure to follow me on social media, so you know when I post a new vlog or go live." As I speak in my usual high-energy voice, things feel normal for the first time in a long time.

I keep the momentum going. "I want to do things different tonight. I know I've been doing a lot of videos about the cult. Right now, though, my brain just needs to shut off and do something fun. I have the text-to-voice and video donations on. Like always, you don't have to donate, but it helps pay the bills, seeing how vlogging is my full-time job. Let's find something to play and get started."

Two hours go by. The fans and I have been gaming together, shooting the shit and having a lot of fun with each other. Aside from the few trolls that come with these live streams, things have been great. "Guys, I just want to say thank you very much for this," I tell them sincerely. "This whole cult thing has been taking over my life, and I needed this to take my mind off things and just turn my brain off."

A five-dollar text-to-voice donation appears on the screen. It comes from someone whose user name is name up of random numbers and letters. "Thank you for spreading the word of Rajachar. Praise be to the Rajachar. Praise be to The Great Void," says the generic robotic voice that speaks when someone makes a text-to-voice donation.

I laugh, thinking it's just a random troll. "Hilarious. Thank you for the money. It'll go towards the groceries that I need to buy soon."

Another five-dollar donation comes in from a different user whose user name is also made up of random numbers and letters. "We saw your videos. They are masterpieces. Rajchar is smiling upon you." In the back of my head, I wonder if this is just some terrible joke, or if this is really the cult. They've got the name wrong, so it's probably not the cult. But I've grown nervous, and decide that I should stop the stream.

I clap my hands and smile at the camera. "Okay, guys, these people here have ruined it for everyone, so I'll call it here. Like I said, be sure to follow me on social media, and I'll talk to you guys later." I log off of the live stream.

Shaking my head, I get up and head to the kitchen to pour myself a cup of coffee. I take a sip and wonder if I was being trolled, or if the donations really were from members of the cult. Shaking my head, I walk over and sit back down in front of the computer. Just then, a window appears on the screen showing me I'm getting a call. The contact information fields contain only random numbers and letters. I double-click on the screen to answer it. "Hello?"

When I answer the video call, all I see on-screen is a person in an emerald-green mask. It matches the one from the video with Kimberly's death. I sit there like a deer in headlights, frozen in fear. My mind races, trying to figure out how they even got ahold of my info to call me. I swallow the huge lump of fear in my throat and demand, "How did you get my contact information? I don't give this out to anyone but close friends."

The person in the mask starts typing on the keyboard. "We have our ways," appears in the chat box.

"What do you want from me?"

After I ask, the figure types on the keyboard more. "I want you to come to LA."

I'm confused at the response. "LA? What's in LA?" I ask, hoping I won't get some cryptic answer.

I do. "Booze and Boobs."

The expression on my face goes from confusion to *what the fuck?* While I sit there at a loss for what to do, the person under the mask starts laughing hysterically. "Okay, okay, I'm sorry, J!" He takes off the mask, still laughing.

It's fucking Kyle fucking Denney. He's another vlogger I've collaborated with from time to time. I sigh in relief, sinking in my chair, relaxing upon seeing a familiar face. "Fuck you!" I snap.

Kyles laughter slowly tapers off, but he still has this massive grin on his face. "Sorry, man, I had to. I've been following your stuff. I caught the tail-end of your live stream. I was bored, and well," he holds up a bottle of beer for me to see. "Kinda drunk." He takes a swig from the bottle. "Look, like I said, I've been following your vlogs about this cult. That's some deep stuff you found."

"Yeah, no shit. So what's up? " I ask him.

"Look, you've been freaking the fuck out. So I'm flying you out to L.A. to get you drunk and laid. You'll have a really good time," Kyle says enthusiastically.

I shake my head. "I just got done paying rent and bills—"

Kyle cuts me off mid-sentence. "Didn't you hear me!?" he asks me, still enthusiastic "*I* will fly you out. Plus, I have an extra room at my place. Don't worry about anything. I got it taken care of. I'll pick you up at the airport, bro!"

I smile at him, knowing he means well. "Kyle, thanks for the offer, but...."

He cuts me off once more. "Okay, I'll end this talk right here. I already bought your ticket. Check your email." I check my email, and sure enough, there's a receipt for a plane ticket purchased by Kyle for me.

I look at him sarcastically. "Well, look at that. It's a plane ticket for tomorrow. I'm so surprised."

He smiles. "A plane ticket!? You must've won a contest or something. I'll be there to pick you up at the airport."

Kyle ends the call, and I mutter, "Guess I'd better get packing."

Chapter 9

I stand in baggage claim waiting for my suitcase. I only have two bags with me: my laptop bag, which was my carry-on, and my suitcase containing my clothes. When it comes around on the carousel, I grab the suitcase and hurry outside to wait for Kyle to pick me up. After five minutes of waiting, a black SUV pulls up and Kyle gets out. He trots over to me, smiling wide, his arms out, wanting a hug. "What's up, fucker!?" he says to me enthusiastically.

We meet each other halfway and share a bro-hug. "Here, let me get your bags," he tells me. "Go ahead and get in the car."

"Thanks, man. Long flight." I get in the front passenger seat while he puts my stuff in back of the sleek SUV.

Once everything's loaded, he gets in, and we pull out before the airport cops can bitch at us. "Man, it's good to see you!" he says. His grin is infectious.

"Yeah, it's great to be back here in L.A. I think the last time we hung out in person was that meet-up here, what, about six months ago? "

"That sounds about right. You need to pack up your stuff and move here, ya know? We have these things called *seasons* here. I don't know if you've heard of those in Houston."

I shake my head and laugh. "Nah, I'm doing fine in Houston. We have seasons too. Hot, Hell, Rain, and then about two weeks of winter. A whole month if we're lucky."

"Suit yourself, man," Kyle chuckles. Then he boasts, "Dude, my career has really taken off lately! Things have been so good that I was able to buy my own house. It's great! Nice one-story place. Three bedrooms in the back. In front of the house, I've transformed the garage into a den with a lounge/bar area. Oh, oh, oh, and that's not the best part!" He glances over at me, smiling proudly. "In-ground pool and a deck with a hot tub!"

I pat him on the shoulder, smiling and happy for him. Although he reminds me of your stereotypical frat guy, he's a good person. "Congrats on the house."

"Thank you, thank you. That means a lot coming from one of my good friends. I never wanted to work some regular nine-to-five, ya know. I wanted to do something different. Something I enjoy doing and get paid to do. My next goal is to do a podcast and get other creators on there."

"Well, you have the face for it."

He laughs with me, then adopts a smug look. "You're right. So, how are things in the house *you* bought?"

I roll my eyes. "Touché."

He merges onto the freeway. "Well, what about you?" he asks.

"What about me?"

"I mean, all this. This cult stuff, man. Look, I thought you were doing it for views and shit. More than half the people who do those 'deep-web mystery boxes' are full of crap. But the more I watched your videos, the more I wondered, 'Damn, is this shit for real?'"

"Hell yes, it's for real," I blurt. "Wouldn't you want to know if there's a serial killer cult that the police aren't telling the public about?"

Kyle shrugs. "Yeah, of course. All I'm saying is, watch yourself. You could be next, bro."

I turn to look at him and sigh deeply. "Thanks, Kyle, but I haven't been completely honest. *I* didn't order the box off the deep web. A good friend or mine named Bret did — and what he ordered got him killed. They found him dead, stabbed, covered in his own blood and fucking candle wax. On top of that, some people with the government came by and asked me some questions. They said they were from some agency called 'United States Special Security' that I don't think really exists. They knew everything about me —full name, birthday, parents, where I went to elementary school, first kiss, hell, even my credit score. Something's fucked up here. I want to know what happened to Bret, so I'm using my social media influence to draw them out and get answers."

Kyle says flatly, "I think you should stop, Jeff. Right away. You have a death-cult interested in you, and now the government's involved. Must be something major if the Feds are knocking on your door."

"Couldn't stop even if I wanted to, man. I'm already in way too deep. Like I said earlier. if there was a serial killer cult running around, wouldn't you want to know about it?" I turn my head away, studying the view outside the SUV's window.

After about an hour of driving, we make it to Kyle's new crib, a nice, modern place home in a decent part of town. We grab my bags, and he escorts me to the room I'll stay in. As we walk through the house, I look around. The interior decor is modern — lots of blacks, whites, and reds, with a dark brown hardwood floor. He opens the door to my room, which has a king-sized bed. Plenty of room for lots of fun. There's also a computer desk more than large enough for me to set up my laptop and peripherals, and a window with a view of the hot tub and pool Kyle had bragged about. The room even has its own bathroom.

"Well, here's your home away from home," Kyle says as he presents it to me. "You need anything, just ask. There'll be a low-key get-together later. It starts at 8, and you'll be there."

I laugh. "Not like I have a say in the matter, seeing as how the place I'm crashing is where it's being held."

With his right index finger, Kyle taps the side of his head, smiling at me, and then points his finger at me as he continues smiling. "Sir, you are correct. Anyway, I'll be in the living room if you need me." As Kyle walks away, leaving me alone in the room. I figure I'll unpack and get settled in.

First, though, I step over to the window to look at the backyard he hyped. It doesn't look half-bad. Nice-sized pool. Hot tub that sits on a wooden deck covered by a wooden awing. It even has a nice sitting area, with a black porch set with a red-brick firepit. I nod appreciatively as I continue scanning the area.

Until I see, standing next to a tree, a tall figure in an emerald-green hooded cloak, wearing an emerald-green mask.

Without thinking about the consequences, or worrying what might happen once I confront the bastard, I rush through house like a madman, bumping into Kyle along the way. I burst through the door to the backyard, rushing outside.

The person in the green cloak is gone.

Kyle rushes outside, a look of confusion on his face. "Dude, what the fuck!?"

"I saw someone!" I yell. Frantically, I start searching all over the backyard for the unwanted guest.

Kyle follows me around, still confused. "What the hell are you talking about?"

"A cult member was standing right near your deck!" I reply, still searching.

Kyle walks over to me and grabs me by the shoulders. "Stop! Dude, look at yourself! You're freaking out. You're seeing shit that isn't there. Most likely you've been losing sleep, right?"

"Look, you're right about the sleep part, but I know what I saw," I tell him, fiercely and confidently.

"Then where is this person, bro?"

I paused and looked around, seeing no one back here but Kyle and I. "Fuck," I mutter under my breath. We both start making our way back in the house. *Am I going insane? I know what I saw. It was* right there, I tell myself.

Kyle pats my back. "Look, you just need to chill. Let's head inside and order some food for later. But you need to stop with this cult stuff, man. It's killing you."

Chapter 10

I sit handcuffed to a metal desk bolted to the floor in a small, windowless interrogation room with bare white walls. The only other thing in here is a black, rolling office chair. I panic, not understanding how I ended up here. The last thing I remember is being with Kyle and three of his friends, sitting around the firepit, talking and having a few drinks. After a while, I got tired and went to bed. And then...

The door opens; a middle-aged white man in a brown suit walks in, carrying a file folder and two bottles of water. He sits down in the office chair and rolls up to the desk, setting down the folder and bottles and its brushed-steel surface. "How you doing, Mr. Bailey? My name is Bill Nickels, and I'm the detective assigned to your case. I brought you some water. If you need anything else, let me know," he tells me in a friendly tone. Good Cop.

I start speaking a mile a minute as the memories flood in on me. "Look, I don't know what happened! We were just hanging out last night. I go to bed, and the next morning I wake up and walk into the living room. Two of Kyle's friends are dead, and Kyle and his other friend are missing!"

After I spill my guts to him, he just nods, not saying anything. He opens the folder and glances at it. Before closing it, he takes out a piece of paper. "Slow down, Jeffery. Let's figure all this out. I want to assure you that my goal is to find out what happened, so that we go down the right path to get you taken care of." He slides a piece of paper and pen over to me. "This is a waiver of rights, NOT an admission of guilt. This just speeds up the process of you telling me your side of things. You seem to be a trustworthy person with nothing to hide. I want you taken care of, so we get you on your way ASAP."

I review the document. I'm pretty good at legalese. The first thing that I notice is that I'm giving up my right to a lawyer. This worries me, but I know I didn't kill those people. Then it hits me like a ton of bricks: Kyle's friends were found with candle wax on their bodies, killed by multiple stab wounds, and before I could say or do anything, the SWAT team busted down the door with their guns drawn and took me here.

I looked at the cop and then back at the paper. I grab the pen and quickly sign it. I have nothing to hide, and now I can spread the word about this cult.

Nickels takes the paper and puts it in the folder. "Take your time, relax, and start talking when you're ready," he said, leaning back in his chair.

"I already know what happened."

"Please go right ahead," he says.

"This is gonna sound crazy, but there's this serial killer cult out there. I got my hands on a package from the deep web. In it, there was this thumb drive with a video of people getting killed. When I found out what was on it, I turned it in to the police. Later, I found out it was a cult that killed the people on the video. Some of their sacrifices were volunteers, some weren't. Apparently they've been doing this for years for something the call Rojachar. I've been vlogging about all this lately, and I take it they don't like that. It seems they tracked me down to L.A., where I was visiting with Kyle

Childress. They killed Kyle's friends and kidnapped him and a girl who was with us. Look, we have to track them down — otherwise they'll be sacrificed!" I explain to the detective in a panicked tone.

"Interesting story," the detective says mildly.

I slam my hands down on the desk in frustration at the fact that he obviously doesn't believe me. "It's not just a story! It's the truth!"

The detective doesn't flinch at my outburst. "Anything else you want to share with me?" he asks.

I shake my head and slump. "No, because that's the truth. It's all I got."

He nods. "Okay, you say that's what happened. But here's what *actually* happened, because your story doesn't add up. If there really is a cult that doesn't like you talking about them, then why did they kill and kidnap your friends and leave you alone?"

I say nothing, because it makes little sense. If I'm the one telling the public about them, then why leave me alive? Disinformation?

"You say you were asleep," the cop says, "but how can you sleep through this?" He opens the folder and pulls out two photos of two guys named Dan and Steve, the two friends of Kyle who were at the get-together. They both have stab wounds and black candle wax all over their bodies. "I did some research, Jeffery. You're both vloggers. You got jealous of Kyle, because Kyle had a lot more fans than you. More views than you. Way more money than you. We have the data to back it up."

I kick the table in anger at what he says. "That's bullshit! Kyle and I were friends!"

Before I can say another word, he cuts me off. "Stop. See? That's what happened." Nickels leans in close. "You got mad then, too. As the night went on, you had a few drinks, and then a few more drinks. You knew Kyle's content was better than yours. It pissed you off that he was more popular than you. The alcohol got the best you. It happens to the best of us, and that's okay," he said in a soothing tone. He taps his fingers on the picture so I look at it. "In a drunk and blind rage, you grabbed a knife. Two of his friends tried to calm you down. When they tried to take the knife away, you stabbed them.

After them, you stabbed Kyle and his other friend. You hid Kyle and his friend's bodies. Next, you poured candle wax on the first two you killed and blamed this cult. From your vlogs." He said "cult" and "vlogs" using air quotes. "You get ready to leave the scene, but the police arrive and catch you before you got away. We got the call from Kyle's neighbor. She said she heard a helluva fight."

He points his fingers at the pictures of the dead bodies as he stares at me. "We have two dead boys and two missing bodies that" he points at me with his index finger,"—you know the location of."

I frantically shake my head. "That didn't happen! The cult!"

The detective cuts me off. "Jeffery, just stop." He rolls his chair closer to me and puts his hand on my back, trying to comfort me.

"Look, I'm not the bad guy here," I say in a defeated tone.

"No, you aren't a bad guy. You got drunk. You got pissed. I'm trying to help you out here. Come clean and tell me what happened, and I can make sure you're taken care of."

I sit there, hunched over, going over everything in my head. I begin to wonder. *Did I get drunk and kill everyone? Kyle does have*

75

more fans than me. I mean, I want those fans. More fans mean more money and opportunities. I have bills to pay just like everyone. I clench my fist. *Bragging about his fucking house.* I take a deep breath and tell Nickels, in a defeated tone, "Okay. Here is what I think might have happened..."

Before I can say anything more, there's a knock on the door, and the two government agents who visited my apartment days before enter the interrogation room. Nickels sits straight up with a surprised look on his face and demands, "Can I help you two?".

"Yes, Detective," the female agent states. "I'm Special Agent Rebecca Hayes, and this my partner, Special Agent Gordon Miller," and they brandish their badges at Detective Nickels. "We're from the United States Special Security Agency. Division of the NSA."

"Special Security? Never heard of it." The detective gets up and makes a shooing motion. "Now, 'Special Agents,' if you'll wait outside, I'll be more than happy to help you later." The agents don't move an inch.

"If we leave, we're taking your prisoner with us." Miller points at me.

Nickels glances at me and then back at the agent, and chuckles a bit, shaking his head. "That's not happening. He's the prime suspect in two murder cases and two missing persons cases." He motions toward me. "He was just about to confess."

Miller smiles. "But he didn't, did he? So as far as we all know, the killer's still out there."

"We need your suspect for reasons of national security," Hayes adds.

Nickels looks at them, confused. "Bullshit. What do you mean, national security?!" he snaps.

"We can't tell you the details. It's classified," Hayes replies.

The all look to the door as a tall, heavyset man in a police uniform walks in. It's getting crowded in the interrogation room. "Chief Smith? What's going on?" Nickels asks.

"Let him go, Detective," Chief Smith says wearily.

"But Chief, he was about to—"

"*Now*, Detective Nickels," Smith orders sternly. "I don't like it any more than you do, but they're legit and the have the authority to take the case *and* the suspect away from us."

Begrudgingly, Nickels complies and uncuffs me. Miller smiles. "Thank you, Detective."

The detective says nothing, just glares at the agents.

Miller looks at me. "Let's go, kid. We got stuff to do." I quickly get up and leave the room. Before we leave the station, we stopped at the front and get my things. The USSSA agents put me in a black sedan, in a backseat caged like a cop car's, and we pull out. The first thing I notice in the backseat with me is my luggage. "Why and how are bags here?" I ask loudly. "They were at Kyle's place."

Hayes peers over her shoulder from the front passenger seat. "Don't worry about it. We got you covered, Jeffery,"

I wilt with relief. "Thank you. Thank you so much. I don't know what happened. I was sleeping, and woke up to dead bodies and police busting in on me." They don't respond, and I ask the most important of many questions whirling through my mind: "Where are we going?"

"LAX," Miller replies from the driver side. "Getting you back home. Or we can take you back to the police station if you prefer."

"Airport works. So just what are you guys, anyway? What's Special Security, really?"

"The agency that saved you from a life sentence for murder," Hayes says laconically.

"What about my friend Kyle?" I ask.

"Local police will stay on the case." Miller replies.

I lean back in my seat. "So... why did you get me out?"

"No more talking." Miller says sharply.

I roll my eyes and sigh, then look out the window and cross my fingers, hoping Kyle is okay.

After about an hour of driving in the hellish traffic, we finally up to the drop-off area at LAX. Hayes glances at me. "Check your email; your ticket's there."

I take out my phone and check my email, and yeah, there's a ticket home in my inbox. First class. "Better go catch your flight," Miller says.

So I grab my bags and get out the car. Once I'm out, the car pulls away. I sigh heavily and walk into the airport, looking for the nearest bar.

Chapter 11

It's only been a day since I got home from L.A. I hang around my apartment, half-stunned, just trying to get a grip on what's happened. I've tried calling, texting, and emailing Kyle, and there hasn't been a response. Is he dead? Worse, is he a member of the fucking cult? Did he lure me to L.A. on purpose just to shut me up? I don't intend to shut up, but since I've been home. all I've really been doing is pacing around my apartment trying to figure out what to do next.

I hear a knock on my door, and it jangles my nerves. Not knowing who it could be, I panic and rushed to the kitchen to grab a chef's knife. Then I walk over to my phone to open the app to look through the camera on the doorbell. I sigh in relief, seeing that it's just a delivery person. "It must be that graphics card I ordered last week," I mutter. Still paranoid, I have the knife in my hand as I walk to the door. I cracked open the door just enough so that the delivery guy sees me without a knife in my hand. I sign for my package before he gives it to me and leaves, and that's that.

I close the door and lock it, trying to calm myself down. The first thing I notice is that the package is way too small for a graphics card, so no telling what it really is. I also notice that there's no return address. Feeling uneasy, I use the kitchen knife cut open the package. Inside is a thumb drive. I stare at it, very confused and very scared. "What the hell?"

After a long while, I walk over to my desk, worried and frightened at what might be on it, considering the last thumb drive I received unsolicited, and power off my Internet router before plugging the drive into my computer. Once plugged in, I run a scan on it, making sure there isn't anything on the drive that can damage my computer. No viruses or malware, so that's a good start. I double-click to open it, and there's just one video file on the drive, titled *Watch Me*. Fuck, not again. I swallow the lump of fear in my throat before double-clicking on the file to open it.

My eyes widen in fear at what I see. It's a wide shot of an unconscious Kyle and Macy, the girl who went missing with him.

They're both naked and tied to wooden chairs, the old, sturdy kind, located in some vast, dimly lit, dingy place that looks like a warehouse. They both start to slowly regain consciousness. Once they wake up, they look around frantically, yelling for help, struggling to get free.

"Shhhhhh," a female voice hisses off-camera.

"Who *are* you!?" Macy shrieks in fear.

"Shhhh, it's okay, Macy. You'll be in a better place soon."

A person in a green hooded cloak and green mask walks into the frame and begins stroking Kyle's head lovingly. Kyle furiously moves his head away with each stroke.

"Who are you? Where are we?" Macy yells as she starts to cry.

The cloaked figure looks at Macy, and when she speaks, I can all but hear her smug smile. "I'm the person who will make you one with The Great Void," she explains cockily. "As for where we are, don't worry about it — you won't be here for much longer."

The cloaked figure walks away from Kyle and stands in the middle of the camera frame. "We know you're watching, Jeffery dear. Don't worry about how we sent this. We are everywhere and everyone. We are your friends. We are your neighbors. We are the rich. We are the poor. We all make choices. We all know what it's like to clearly see the corruption of the world. To see the rich get richer and the poor get poorer. It's okay, though. Thanks to you and the Great Void, we can build a better world. One world, one mind, for a better future. You are doing His work, Jeffery. You are doing His will. All you have to do is join us, and we can usher in a new world. Join us." She walks closer to the camera. "Join us. Your friends will soon join The Great Void. You can, too."

"What are you talking about, you crazy fuck?" Kyle shouts.

"Haven't you been watching Jeffery's vlogs?" The cloaked figure turns around. "If not, you'll find out soon. Everything will become clear to you."

Two other cloaked figures, this time wearing black hoods, step into the frame. One holds a large medical tray. On it are two closed Mason jars, a knife, tweezers, a needle, and thread. The green-cloaked figure grabs one of the jars and holds it up in front of the camera to show that there are dead flies inside. "When people don't understand his love, we *make* them understand. He speaks to them through lesser beings, and then they understand his will. You use harsh words like slavery or brainwashing. We call it unwavering faith."

She walks over to Kyle with the knife. Kyle struggles even harder to get free the closer she gets. Using the knife, she cuts his arm just enough to have blood run down his arm. She collects enough blood in the jar to cover the flies, and repeats the process with Macy with the other jar. "He knows who you are now," she says in a loving tone.

She sits the knife down on the medical tray, and holds both the Mason jars with the flies high in the air. She and the other two cloaked figures look up at the jars. "Praise The Great Void! Praise Rojachar!" she shouts. The other two cloaked figures repeat after her, simultaneously. Then she continues, "Great Void, we come to you so you may speak to these disbelievers! Make them understand that you are coming, so you can bring an age of peace! Speak to them so that they will know your love, will have unwavering faith in you, and will live to serve you! Praise Rojachar!"

"Praise Rojachar," the other two repeat fervently.

She sits the two jars back down on the medical tray, and all three of them then walk over to Kyle. She unscrews the jars and then grabs the pair of tweezers. Very carefully, she reaches into a jar to grab hold of a fly. She removes it from the jar and looks at Kyle. Kyle turns to look back at her, struggling even harder than previously. "What are you doing, you sick fucks?!" he roars. "Let me go!"

"We are awakening you to his love," the priestess replies in a motherly tone. One of the cloaked figures grabs Kyle's head, holding it as tight as if were in a vise. Macy screams louder for help. The only reply she gets is her own voice echoing back at her. With Kyle's head held tight, the priestess places the blood-covered fly inside his ear. Then, using a hooked needle and catgut, then sews his ear shut with quick, surgical movements, trapping the fly inside. She repeats the process with Kyle's other ear, before doing the same to Macy's ears.

Both their screams and cries for help echo back them, unanswered.

The three cloaked figures step back and just stare at Kyle and Macy.

Macy breaks and starts crying in earnest. "Please, please, let us go! We promise we won't tell anyone. Please, just let us go!"

"You people are fucking sick!" Kyle yells at them. "Why the fuck would you put dead bugs *inside* someone?!"

Before anyone can say anything else, Macy lets out a blood-curdling scream. "They're moving! I can feel it! They're trying to get into my head!" She emits another scream. Not long after, Kyle shakes his head violently, yelling and doing whatever he can to get the flies out. He slams his ears against his shoulders, hoping it will kill them. This goes on for about five minutes before they both slowly stop fighting to get free. Once they've stopped fighting, they're left with far-off expressions on their faces, just staring off into nothing.

"Speak," the woman in the green cloak orders them.

"Praise Rojachar," Kyle and Macy replied in monotones.

"Pure, unwavering faith," says the priestess. She steps in front of the camera and stares at it, at me; and as she does, I feel a deep sense of dread, as if this is live and she's staring into my soul. "People fear what they don't understand," she says in an eerily reasonable voice. "But soon they *will* understand, and it will all be because of you. Join us and let us help you. Join us."

"Join us." one cloaked figure in the background says, echoed by the other. Then Macy and Kyle repeated the chorus.

A chill sweeps through my body as someone or something whispers "Join us" in my ear.

I shoot up out of my chair, knocking it back, and grab the knife I used to open the package. I back myself against the wall and survey my living room. There's no one here but us chickens, it seems, but I'm not sure I believe that. I rushed into my bedroom, open the nightstand desk, and grabbed a 9 mm Glock, which I have never fired except at a range. Once. I thumb the safety off and chamber a round, then rush around all over my one-bedroom, one-bathroom apartment, searching for the whisperer.

It's all clear.

Breathing a sigh of relief, I reengage the safety on the pistol and walk over my desk, to sit down and just think about everything I just saw. An idea comes to mind. I search around on my desk, and it doesn't take me long to find what I'm looking for: Miller's card. When he picks up, I blurt, "Agent Miller? It's me, Jeffery Bailey. You and your partner helped me out in L.A. Hey, I just got this package in the mail. It's a thumb drive with a video on it of what happened to Kyle Childress and his girlfriend Macy... An hour? Yeah, I'll see you then."

When Miller and Hayes arrive, still all in black, we sit in my living room and watch the video. "Is this all they sent you?" Miller asks after it cuts off.

"Yeah, that's all, nothing else. How long have you guys known about this cult?"

"A very long time," Hayes replies wearily.

"So why haven't you taken them down yet?" I ask.

She looks at me with hard eyes. "We have. We've taken down various small groups associated with the cult. But as soon as one group goes down, another pops up. There have been Rojachar cult activities in England, Russia, and other parts of Europe, not just the U.S. Most of the major activity is here in the States, though. We know there's a hierarchy. Like the girl in the video said, they're everyone. We've arrested everyday 9-to-5 factory workers, business drones on the Fortune 500, and everyone in between. Most of the time, the cult has remained low on the radar, but two years ago they started racking up their kill count. They're doing this for a reason."

"We need to figure out why, and fast," Miller adds.

"That's where you come in, Jeffery," Hayes says to me, sliding over a piece of paper.

"What's that?" I point at the paper.

"An agreement, stating that you will cooperate with us until the end of this investigation, or until we release you from this agreement, whichever happens first. It also states that once the investigation is done, you can't talk about the investigation or us. Once you're done, we will compensate you handsomely for your time."

I glance down at the paper and then back up at them. "What do you need me to do?"

"Just keep doing what you're doing now. Get their attention. They haven't killed you for a reason. They could have."

I look down at the paper, and figure this could get me one step closer to finding out what happened to Bret. I sign the agreement and looked at them. "So, how much are you paying me?"

Chapter 12

My new coworkers leave after they've gotten everything squared away. I head over to my computer and sit down, preparing for a surprise live stream. I figure this will draw out some cult members. "I'll just do something easy," I mutter. "Play some games, talk to people, see what happens." It doesn't take me long to set up. I post on my various social media accounts to spread the word that I'll be live-streaming within the hour.

As the live-stream begins, people trickle in. "Hey everyone, what's up," I say when I hit a critical number. "Jeffery B. here. I wanted to do a live-stream. Nothing special — we're just going to just hang out and have fun and play some video games. I know a lot of you want updates on the cult stuff. I'll just say that the police came to talk to me, and there's a big investigation going on. I can't say much more without getting into trouble."

The live stream goes on for about an hour before a voice-to-text donation comes in from someone whose username is a stream of random numbers and letters. The robotic voice says, "The Void Mother will soon give birth to Rojachar here on earth."

"You know, I keep hearing about this Rojachar. Who the hell is Rojachar?" I ask.

Another donation comes in from the same person. "Rojachar is a deity who will bring order to the chaos on this plane of existence, by swallowing this planet and ushering in an age of peace. Soon everyone will embrace him, whether they want to or not."

If it weren't for everything that I've been through, I'd call this person crazy.

A light bulb flips on in my head. "Wait, wait, wait a minute here. How the hell do I know this is really someone from the cult? How do I know this isn't some troll? Someone trying to get a rise out of me?" I ask, a smug, confident look on my face, trying to keep cool; but underneath, I'm praying that this *is* just some troll. The chat goes on, some watchers saying that it's a troll, some people saying that it really is a cult member. There are also people claiming all of this is some game I made up. That goes on for about two minutes before another donation comes in; this time it's a video donation. On the screen is the last view seconds of the video from the latest thumb drive — the part where they're demanding I join them. I freak out, knowing that this person is the real deal.

"What do you guys want from me?" I demand, my face livid with fear.

Another video donation comes in. On-screen is Kyle, his face expressionless, almost like he's dead. "We want you to take your place with us, Jeffery," he says.

After that, I feel an impossible breeze pass through my apartment, and my power flickers a bit before returning to normal. I look around nervously, and without saying goodbye, I log off the live-stream.

I turn and see Bret standing there, naked, covered in blood and black candle wax, blood still pouring from his stab wounds. "Join us," he says, reaching out to me. I scream in fear and run to my room, where I grab my gun from the nightstand and then rush back into the living room — only to find that nothing is there. I look around my apartment cautiously, unable to find anyone else or signs of anyone else here but me. "What the hell is going on?" I croak.

94

After I finish looking around my apartment, I grab a bottle of whiskey and a drinking glass, and fill the glass a quarter full. I gulp the whiskey and then pour another glass and take another drink. "That couldn't have been real," I groan. "I have to be seeing shit."

No response. So far, so good. "Okay, focus. That *wasn't real*. Just stress and lack of sleep. That all that was," I say, trying to convince myself. I pour myself another stiff drink and down it before heading over to my computer and sitting down in front of it. "Okay, who or what is The Void Mother?" I ask myself. I start searching the regular web to see if I can get lucky before I have to look through the labyrinth of the deep web.

I start on the site where I normally post my vlogs. To my surprise, when I type *Void Mother* into the search bar at the very bottom of the results page, a video titled, "Where is Tiffany Natts?" pops up. Turns out a vlogger I follow made the video. She mainly posts true crime stuff. One tag she for this post used was "Void Mother."

I click on the video, and it starts playing. It begins like every other video, with the vlogger asking her fans to make sure they follow their social media pages and blah blah blah. "This is Tiffany Natts," the vlogger says as a picture of Tiffany comes up on the screen. She has brown hair that goes down to her shoulders; she looks fit and healthy. Even has a cute smile. "At the time of this video, Tiffany is 23 and has been missing for a year and a half. She is a vlogger who also posted on this site." A video clip of Tiffany cooking comes up on screen. "Her vlogs focused around cooking, meal prep, and promoting healthy eating habits."

More random clips from Tiffany's vlog come onto the screen. "Tiffany Natts was born March 3, 1997 in Phoenix, Arizona. Cooking was Tiffany's passion. Her overall goal was to have a major cooking show on one of the food channels and publish a cookbook. Tiffany got along with everyone. Her bubbly personality drew people to her. Her home life was great. She has two loving parents and a younger sister. Everyone got along great in the family. There was nothing but love in that house.

"About two months prior to her disappearance, things started to change. No longer was she making videos about cooking. She was making videos about her not "belonging" anywhere. Here's an example." A video of Tiffany comes on screen. She wears a baggy pink hoodie, and no makeup. Her hair is tied up in a ponytail. She looks at the camera with a noticeably forced smile. "Hey guys, it's me Tiffany," she says in a defeated and saddened tone. She takes a deep breath and continues. "I know it's been a while since I posted a video or anything on social media. I have seen you all reaching out to me asking if I'm okay. First off, thank you all for looking out for me, and I love you all for it. Lately, I just haven't been feeling myself. I love cooking and sharing my food with all of you. I just have a lot on my mind. I feel like there's this huge piece of me missing. I don't know what that piece is, but I have to find it. So I'll have to leave so I can come back stronger and better for you guys."

The other vlogger is back on the screen. "This was very odd and out of character for Tiffany. A month went by until her next video. During that time, things got even stranger. Friends and family say that she became very distant and was keeping to herself, which was not like her at all. The day she went missing, she posted the following video."

On the screen is Tiffany. Her makeup and hair are done perfectly. She's in a conservative black dress. She has a smile that could light up a room on her face.

"Hi, everyone, I hope you're all having a great day!" Tiffany says in an upbeat and joyful manner that mirrors one of her regular cooking vlogs. "Wow! I don't know if this is goodbye or see you later." She shakes her head. "No, this is 'I'll see you later.' I have found where I belong. I have found my calling in life." She looks down at her stomach and smiles, then looks back at the camera. "I will be a mother. I will be a mother to a Great Void that will swallow this world whole, and because of that, will make a world a happier place. No more crime. No more corruption. No more pain or suffering. We will all be one. We will all know total happiness."

She's was saying all this in a warm, caring tone, like she truly believes in what she's saying. "I know this must sound crazy right now, and it's perfectly fine that you feel that way. To be honest, if I were you, *I* would feel that way. Don't worry, guys, you will all understand soon. This isn't goodbye. This is definitely I will see you later. See you later in the new world." She looks down at her stomach and caresses it, smiling lovingly and proudly. She looks up at the camera, and her smile grows as the video ends.

The vlogger takes the screen once more. "After posting her last video, Tiffany was seen at a series of ATMs cleaning out her entire bank account. All her social media has been silent since. No more activity on her bank account or credit cards. When the police went to her apartment, everything was fine. It didn't look like she had packed her bags, and she left her cellphone behind."

I glance down at *my* cellphone to see if everything is fine on the doorbell camera. Everything looks normal, so I focus my attention on the video. "When police went through her phone records," the vlogger notes, "they found she was speaking regularly with someone by the name of Duke. No one on her social media friends lists had that name. None of her friends knew who Duke was. No pictures of him. Duke's phone number traced back to one of those prepaid burner phones. Tiffany's family is still very hopeful that she will return home safe and sound. If you have any information that could lead to the whereabouts of Tiffany Natts, please call the Phoenix, Arizona police department. Thank you for your time, everyone, and stay safe."

The video ends. I open another browser window and do a search for Tiffany Natts. All that comes up are news articles and other things related to her disappearance. I take my search to the deep web, where I search for "The Void Mother." To my surprise, I come across a website of interest. The site is basic: just a black background with emerald green text, clearly posted by the cult:

Praise the Voice of the Void. He is the Chosen. He will spread the word of the Void. He will lead the faithful into the new world. Once in the new world, the Voice of the Void will lead on the right side of the Great Void, ensuring that the faithful remain faithful.

Praise the Void Mother. It is through her that The Great Void will manifest on Earth and will be able to shed his mortal shell. Because of her, the Great Void will swallow the Earth and bring about a new world of peace and harmony. The Void Mother

100

will rule on the left side of the Great Void, ensuring

that no one will want or need for anything, making

sure that everything is provided for all.

Praise the Great Void, stuck in a veil between

this plane of existence and another. He spoke to the

first Voice of the Void and said, "Fear me not. I am

Rojachar. You will be my voice. Through you, your

people will understand my intentions for this world.

One mind, one thought, living in peace and harmony.

"I will leave the veil and will enter your plane

of existence. I will first enter this world unaware of

who I once was, but over time, I will become aware.

On the first day of my 20th year on Earth, I will shed

my mortal skin and enter the cosmos. From there, I

will devour planet after planet, star system after star

system, galaxy after galaxy. Once I have devoured

everything, once we all have a single mind, all will

know peace. And I will bring this plane of existence

into mine, merging them together and bringing peace

to both.

Chapter 13

About an hour goes by after I find the site on the deep web. I take a screenshot of the web page, along with the URL, which consists of random letters and numbers, and send both to my government handlers. After that's done, I get up from my desk and head to the kitchen to make myself an oven-baked pizza. Later, I walk back over to my desk and sit down. My phone is still plugged into the charger with the screen still on camera view outside my apartment. "Still nothing. Good."

I set a 30-minute alarm for my pizza. To pass the time, I decide to post a video.

"Hey guys, Jeffery B. here. I figured I'd give you guys an update on what's been going on lately. We only have 30 minutes. My pizza will be ready soon." I talk about the video I saw about Tiffany Natts and how I think it relates to the cult. I also mention the website I found with what I can only describe as a religious text. The timer on my alarm goes off, letting me know that my pizza is ready. "Okay, guys, that's my pizza. I'm going to go eat. Like always, follow all my social media pages, and I'll see you soon."

I post the video and head for the kitchen, where I use an oven mitt to remove the pizza from the oven. Four quick slashes with the pizza slicer, and it's in eight pieces. I turn the oven off and grab two slices, then return to at my desk. As I take a bite of pizza, I start browsing both the regular web and deep web for more information about that Tiffany Natts chick and the cult.

After a few minutes of searching, my phone makes a sound alerting me that someone's in front of the door, and my doorbell rings soon afterwards. Sighing, I look at my phone to see who's there. It's a brunette girl wearing blue jeans, a gray shirt, tennis shoes, and a backpack. I tap the intercom key. "Can I help you?"

She glances up at the speaker. "Are you Jeffery Bailey?" she asks.

I mute the mic and run to my bedroom, where I retrieve my handgun and turn the safety off. Figuring she's a whacko from the cult, I prepare myself. I take a deep breath to calm my nerves and unmute the mic. "Sorry, you have the wrong apartment. No one by that name lives here," I say, turning to hide my nervousness as I walk back to the living room. I switch my focus between the door and phone screen repeatedly.

She shakes her head. "Look, I'm not part of the cult. I escaped from it," she says to me in a confident tone. "I know about the videos you've made about the cult. It's all true. I need your help, please," she says into the doorbell camera, her voice intense.

I look at her image and take a deep breath. I pace back and forth, wondering what to do next. "How do I know this isn't some trick!" I finally reply, half-panicked.

She loses her cool and yells into the camera. "Look, I promise I'm not part of the cult! Was I? Yes! You just have to trust me! You said you want to stop the cult, right!? I have info that you need to hear!"

I stand there, wondering what to do. Part of me says she's full of shit, but another part's convinced she's telling the truth. "Take off the backpack and open it!" I demand.

She looks confused. "What?"

"Show me what's in the backpack. I want to make sure you don't have a weapon in there. Your pockets, empty them too."

She sighs and quickly shrugs out of the backpack before opening it. All that's in there are clothes. She then empties her pockets. All she has in her pockets are a wallet and a cell phone.

I sigh in relief when I see that she has no weapons on her. "Hang on." I walk over to the door and unlock it. Stepping away from the door, I tell her to come in, gun aimed at the door just in case she has people hiding off-camera.

Startled by the gun pointed in her direction, she jerks her hands up. "Holy shit!"

"Close the door," I order.

She reaches behind her with one hand and closes the door, while keeping the other up in the air.

"Lock it."

She grabs the deadbolt and turns it, then puts her hand back up in the air. "Mind putting the gun down, Mr. Bailey? You're freaking me out," she says tensely.

"In a minute. And it's Jeffery. First, how the hell did you find me?"

"I paid a hacker from the deep web to help me out. With enough cash, you can get anything."

I should have known. "And why did you *need* to find me?"

"Your vlog. You have a large following. I have information that can help you expose this cult for what it is."

I stand there and think for a bit. Then I click the safety on and put the gun down on the desk. She sighs heavily and lowers her hands, relaxing a bit. "What's your name?" I ask flatly.

"Natalie."

"Take a seat, Natalie. Let's figure all of this out." I consider consulting my friends in the government, then decide not to do so right away. I sit at the computer chair and she takes a seat on the couch in front of me. "You said you have information that will help me. Let's hear it."

"It's real. The cult, I mean. A lot more people will die if something isn't done," she warns.

"I know the friggin' cult is real. It's already gotten some of my friends. But what do you mean, a lot more people will die? What are you talking about?"

"This cult is *huge*. It contains people from all walks of life, from every social class. The Order of the Void has the financial means and manpower to pull off anything they feel need to get done—including bribing government officials."

I nod. I've already figured as much. "And do you know who the leader is?" I asked.

"Ever heard of a vlogger named Devin Highmore?"

I draw my head back, a little surprised. "Yeah. I've never watched his content, but I've heard of him. He used to post content about the stock market, and how to make money off it and stuff like that. Got rich from his own advice, and started his own entertainment company, called Highmore Entertainment, I think? He's signed a bunch of other content creators and social media influencers. He even has some actors and musicians working under his brand. I met him at a convention last year. He's a nice guy."

"That's what I thought too, when I first met him," she snarls.

"What does he have to do with all this? Is he the in the cult?"

"The bastard's the *leader* of the cult," she says forcefully.

"Look, just get me in front of a camera, and I'll explain everything. "

Chapter 14

I nod at Natalie as I finish setting up the lighting, and straighten the camera on its tripod, whereupon I walk over to the couch and sit down in the center. "I'll do a quick intro, then I'll get up, okay? Then you can take a seat, and I'll ask you questions. Just answer whatever you can. Sound good?"

She nods. "Got it. Let's get started."

I point to the camera. "On the left side of the camera is the Record button. Press it, and we'll get everything started."

She walks over to the camera and presses the button, then points at me, letting me know the camera is rolling. I look at the camera and give a half-assed wave, as if to say I'm ready for all this to be over — which I am. "Hey everyone, it's Jeffery B. I'm gonna keep this intro short. Right now, I have a person with me who escaped from the cult I've been investigating. It seems that it's called The Order of the Void, which makes sense. I realize some of you may not believe me or her, and honestly, I might not believe it either if I were you. This is some abnormal shit, am I right? But all I'm asking is for you to hear her out." I get up and walk off-camera, sitting down in my computer chair next to the camera.

Natalie takes my place in the center of the couch. I notice that her eyes have bags underneath them, and she looks exhausted. She's still pretty. "Hello, everyone," she says quietly, "my name is Natalie. The cult that Jeffery has been vlogging about is real. I was in it for about three years, and got out recently."

"Let's start from the beginning," I say. "How did you learn about the cult, and what led you to join it?"

"The cult is ancient, but for me, it started three years ago with my best friend Kim. We both lived in an apartment in Queens, New York. She had a job interview at Highmore Entertainment in Manhattan for a graphic designer position. Afterword, she went on and on about how she got the job and even met Devin Highmore himself. She told me he was a nice, charming man. It was him who hired her, not her direct supervisor.

"She explained to me that it wasn't your normal 9-to-5 position; it was something new every day. She even got to work personally with vloggers, influencers, and actual celebrities signed to Highmore. After five months, she started going in really early and staying late. At first, I thought it nothing of it. Then she started to go in on her days off sometimes. I asked her if everything was okay, and she said she wanted the overtime and just really enjoyed her job."

"No red flags or anything for you?" I ask.

She shakes her head. "No, nothing at all. She was my best friend; I didn't see a reason why she would lie. One day, I went by her office and told her I wanted to grab lunch together. The building was this 20-story, emerald-green office building, kind of odd-looking for Midtown. I walked into the building and checked in with the four security men in the front desk. One thing I noticed was that three of them were in your everyday grey security uniform, but the fourth one was in black slacks and an emerald-green, button-down long-sleeved shirt. The man in the button-down did the most talking. He told me to have a seat in the lobby, and that he'd page Kim, letting her know I was there. I took a seat, and I noticed that there were other people in emerald green tops mixed in with people who wore normal business attire."

I have a confused looked on my face. "Why was it that only a few of them wore green tops?"

"To the public, they're managers and other higher-ups within Highmore Entertainment. Within the cult, they're The Enlightened. They're the cult's leaders. I'll go into more detail about them later. Anyway, while I was waiting, Devin showed up. He wore this cheesy smile, almost as if to say, 'I own all of you, and there's nothing you can do about it.' It wasn't pleasant, at least not to me. He shook hands, smiled, and made small talk with everyone he crossed paths with. Treated them like they were his best friends. He walked over to the waiting area I was in, and just like everyone else, started making small talk with me."

"I've only spoken with him in passing for a bit at a convention," I say. "You were around him for three years. What's he like?"

She pauses and looks down, thinking about what to say next, then looks up at the camera. "Charming, intelligent, manipulative.

Evil. He has this aura around him that draws people in. It's hard to explain. We talked for about 15 minutes. I mentioned to him how I was looking for a new job. I told him I wanted to work in public relations, because that's what I went to school for. When I told him that, he acted like I was a godsend. He said he wanted to grow his public relations and marketing teams. He asked me if I was interested in the job, and of course I said yes. He told me to come by the next day to fill out the new hire paperwork. Just like that, I was Highmore's property. The next day, I did all the paperwork, and that's when everything took off for me."

"So you started working for Devin Highmore. What happened next?"

"It started off great. I was using my degree for something that fit my education perfectly. My team worked closely with Kim's team, so I was around my best friend a lot, and we worked smoothly together. I was one of those few people in the world who could say I loved my job and mean it—like the old saying, about how if you find work you love, you'll never work a day in your life. For a while, that was me." She says all this with a growing smile, thinking about the past. "Six months went by. One day, I came home to Kim wearing black slacks and an emerald green button-up top, yelling orders at three men packing up all her belongings, as if she were a drill sergeant in the military. When I asked her what was going on, she told me she'd gotten a promotion, and that she was moving into an apartment building across the street from the office building that Highmore Entertainment owns. It's where most, if not all, of The Enlightened live, as well as some talent in Highmore Entertainment."

"You mentioned The Enlightened before. Who are they and what do they do?" I ask her.

"The cult has a hierarchy," she says, eyes bright. "First, you have acolytes. They're the lowest rank. They're the ones who make sure everything gets done within the cult. All the low-tier work no one would want to do, they do. Think of them as privates in the military. They also make sure the celebrity cult members have everything they need, and I mean *everything*," she emphasized. "Drugs, sex, whatever perversion you can think of. A celebrity member will have a whole personal staff made up of nothing but acolytes to cater to their every whim. And when I say celebrities, I'm not just talking your everyday vloggers with large followings. I'm talking big-time movie icons in big-time movies, TV stars, the best singers—A-list celebrities."

She notices the look of surprise on my face when she mentions that, and nods. "When Devin first started Highmore Entertainment, he was determined to get major celebrities, models, social media influencers, and other people of status to be a part of the organization. His reasoning was to make Highmore Entertainment more prestigious and a great place to work at. It worked well. Thanks to the money and status the celebrities brought in, he was able to fund the activities of the cult, and also open up talent agencies in places all over the country, and recently one in London."

"Do all the members of the cult work for Highmore Entertainment?" I questioned.

She shook her head. "No, but mostly everyone who works for Highmore Entertainment is in the cult. Next, you have Acolyte

Superiors. They make sure the Acolytes are doing what they need to do both in the cult and on the business side of things. Kind of like sergeants, I guess.

"Finally, you have The Enlightened. They're the more radical members — more like the Catholic priesthood than military officers. They're the religious leaders of the cult. Anything problematic, they handle it. They act as judge, jury, and executioner when comes to policing the cult. And I do mean executioners, literally. Whatever an Enlightened tells you to do, you do it. They work extremely close to Devin and only answer to him."

"How does someone become an Enlightened?" I ask, frowning.

"You're chosen by another Enlightened or Devin himself. Besides being higher up in the food chain, you learn more about the deep inner workings of the cult."

"I saw a video with a friend in it," I say, trying to keep my voice from trembling. "The cult members had killed a couple of his friends during a get-together to frame me, then captured my friend and his girlfriend. In the video, they... they cut them, on their arms, then dribbled their blood on these dead flies in jars. Their blood revived the flies. Then they put the flies in their ears and, and *sewed them shut*. After that, they both became mindless zombie for the cult. Can you explain that?" I asked her.

"I don't know how to explain it, but I've seen it before. They perform some type of ritual with the flies, ending just like you've described. They say Rojachar speaks to the unwilling and makes them willing. I don't know how it works, but it does."

"Do you know how long the cult has been around?"

She shakes her head. "No, but I've heard there have been many leaders. As the years progressed, as did the cult. It has its hands in a bit of everything: business, politics, sports, and entertainment. There are families who have been members for generations. Devin brought the cult into the modern age. With social media being a vital part in everyone's life, he knew he could use that as a tool to recruit more people into the cult. It was easy for him. He would find some up-and-coming social media influencer, for example, wine and dine them, groom them for his needs and the cult's, then sign them to Highmore Entertainment. Next he would have them join the cult. From there, he would use that person's following to recruit more people into the cult. "

"And if they don't join the cult?"

"They *all* do. Willingly, or they end up like your friend and become a puppet for the cult. Or they dig deep and blackmail you into signing." She takes a deep breath and sighs. "Do you mind if we take a break?" she asks.

"Not at all." I get up and cut the camera off.

Chapter 15

After about 15 minutes of us talking about anything other than the cult, we get back into it. Natalie takes her seat in the center of the couch, I take my chair, and I press *Record* on the camera. I then ask, "Natalie, you gave us a breakdown of some of the inner workings of The Order of the Void. But what led you to join?"

She sighs. "Kim and I were at lunch one day, and she went on and on about how she'd joined this new religion, The Order of the Void. I was surprised, because she wasn't the religious type. She said The Order was about spiritual growth through bettering society and the people in it, and that it would be the leadership of the Age of the Great Unification. She explained that as an age of no wars or violence or pain; an age of absolute peace. She told me all this with total confidence. She mentioned how they were having a gathering later that night, and asked me to come."

"What happened next?"

"I was hesitant. I thought she was crazy, but Kim and I have known each other since third grade, and I figured she wouldn't put me in a dangerous situation, so I agreed to meet up with her. I just wanted to be a good friend and support her, you know? So later, I met Kim at work. The building was open 24/7, see. There was always some kind of work being done — either cult-related, or some musician working on their music, or something similar. People are always going in and out. She asked if I trusted her, and I told her of course I did.

"We walked in and headed to the very back of the building, into the boiler room. Standing between us and a large set of green metal double doors were these two very large men in black pants and emerald green button-down shirts and a metal detector, like the kind you would see at an airport. Kim took out her employee ID and handed to one of them. He took out a pocketed-sized flashlight and shone a black light on the ID. I couldn't see what he was looking for, but he must have found it. He gave it back and ask who I was, and Kim told them I was a potential new Acolyte. We emptied our pockets and stepped through the metal detector, no problem. The guards opened the doors to this long, ornate hallway with black marble flooring and walls, and low green lighting just bright enough to see by. Down the hallway was another set of double doors with two more people standing guard. We went through the process of them looking at her ID and going through another metal detector. When they opened *those* doors... well, once my eyes adjusted, I was just in shock."

"What was there? What did you see?" I ask eagerly.

"A twisted party. Almost a rave. The room was like a giant two-story ballroom, with the same black marble flooring and walls that were in the hallway. In the center of the room was a circle with a pool of water about knee-deep and about as wide as a large hot tub. It also had three sets of stairs in the floor that led down to the pool. Everyone had on either a black or green cloak with a fancy masquerade ball mask. Also, there were naked men and women walking around serving drinks and appetizers. Every now and then, I would notice one of the cult members walk away with a server to one of the little lounge areas that were spread out throughout the ballroom and..." Natalie paused, a disgusted look on her face... "and

124

get serviced by them. Finally, there were men in emerald green suits just walking around eyeing everything. Most likely security."

"What was running through your mind upon seeing this?"

"I was in shock, scared, confused. I didn't know what to do. We all know the conspiracy theories about how the elite have crazy parties. Parties that include black magic, sex magic rituals, and human sacrifice. But when you see it live and in person..."

"Did you see a lot of that during your time with the cult?"

She tears up and nods. "I was in the cult for three years. After a while, you just get numb to it. I got so numb that it wasn't a big deal. It was as normal as taking out the trash." She buries her face in her hands and just starts sobbing. She cries out "Three years!" as she continues sobbing into her hands. I cut the camera and rush over to comfort her, holding her as she sobs and sobs. Minutes later, she regains her composure, and lets me know that she's ready to start again. I walk back over to the camera and press *Record*. I say nothing. I just point at her and nod, letting her know she's being recorded.

"Kim was talking to a server," she continues. "He walks away, and then comes back with a green cloak and white cloak. Kim put her green one on. I asked her why I needed to put the white cloak on. She told me, 'It's for the ceremony.' I put it on so I won't draw any unwanted attention. She told me the white cloak marked someone just joining the Order of the Void. I told her I wasn't there to join; I was there just to support her. She quickly cut me off and told me that everything would be fine. The lights dimmed, until the only light was the same green light as from the hallway.

"Kim got this huge smile on her face, and told me that the ceremony was about to begin. Everyone gathered around the pool of water in the center. Kim rushed me to the circle in the middle of the room and sat me down in the front row, while she sat behind in the row behind me. Also in the first row were six other people in white cloaks, three men and three women.

"While I sat there, I could see Devin making his way through the crowd. He greeted everyone, shaking hands and giving hugs. He stepped down to the center of the pool of water and greeted all of us in the front row as if we were his best friends." She stopped talking, tearing up again as she remembered.

"And what happened next?" I prompt after a moment.

Natalie clears her throat and replies, "Devin started to speak, and went on about how the reason we were all there was that we wanted a better world. A world of peace. A world free of pain and suffering. I figured he was crazy at first." She paused and looked down at the floor, appearing to be deep in thought for a moment before she looked up at the camera. "But the crazy thing is, he was right — and still is."

"What do you mean?" I ask, surprised.

"We see it every day. Someone does something that should have him in prison for years, but he ends up getting only a slap on the wrist, or worse, gets no time at all because the judge feels that that person 'wouldn't do well in prison.' At the same time, that same judge will give some kid with a non-violent drug charge who was caught with a tiny bit of weed four years in a maximum-security prison, and say people like him are what's wrong with society! It's because of judges like that that my baby brother is dead!" She said this in a voice thick with anger and sadness. "He had just two grams of weed. Two grams of a fucking plant, and was sentenced to a year in prison. A prison where he would die." She said all this while clenching her fists, doing everything in her power to hold back the tears.

"I'm sorry for your loss," I tell her quietly.

She take a deep breath before she starts to speak again. "Thank you. Anyway, they believe that bringing Rojachar into this dimension will bring in this age of total peace. Devin preached about how great Rojachar is, and how great the world will be after Rojachar swallows it. As he spoke, people in black cloaks were filling the circle to the top with water. When he finished speaking, the water was just at the edge of the circle."

"What happened next?"

"When he finished speaking, two people in green cloaks walked in a naked man with a ball gag in his mouth and his hands tied behind his back. When they got him in the water, they forced him to his knees. It took me a second before I realized who it was: Judge Rick Ridgehill, the same bastard who sentenced my brother to prison. Devin said that the judge was in the pocket of those private for-profit prisons. The prison would give him kickbacks for each prisoner he sent their way. My brother was sent to one of those for-profit prisons.

"Three more people in green cloaks entered the pool of water. Two were holding huge chef's knives, practically cleavers, and one held a thick black book about the size of a dictionary. The one with the book held it out to Devin, acting like a human bookstand. Devin started reciting a passage from the large book."

I interject, "What was the book, and what was he saying?"

She shrugs and shakes her head. "I have no idea what's in the book. Only Devin and certain handpicked people can see what's in that book, and they don't speak about it. If I had to guess what it is?" She shrugged. "Maybe a spell book, or a history of the cult. Or both. Like the cult's version of their Bible. As for what he said, I have no idea. He spoke in a language I didn't recognize and had never heard before. It sounded... wrong in a way I can't really describe. Like it wasn't meant for human tongues, or human ears? I couldn't imitate it, or even begin to explain what it sounds like."

I nod sympathetically. "Then what?" I ask.

"As he spoke in this unknown language, other people were chanting 'Praise Rojachar' in sync, while the men with the knives starting making these long, deep cuts on Judge Ridgehill's body. This is when things start to get very strange, and when I knew for sure this was all real and not just some bullshit cult where at the end, the leader asks you to give him all your money."

"What do you mean?"

"It was his blood," she whispers.

"His blood?"

She nods once, sharply. "When his blood touched the water, both started to turn black. Maybe it was just the light, but that's what it looked like. The Devin spoke English again, saying that for his sins, Ridgehill was being baptized and would become one with The Void. The two men who were holding him by his knees dunked him underwater and then pulled him back up. Then it happened: Devin started chanting in that same unknown language. Then he took the knife from one of the two men and just slit Ridgehill's throat. I don't know if it was that the judge was really scared or what, or if Devin just cut really deep, but blood poured from the judge's throat like water from a faucet turned on high. Soon the entire pool was black and murky. It was as if the blood was never red to begin with. The water was completely pitch black. The two men dragged Ridgehill's corpse out like it was a piece of trash. I was pretty much numb, thinking maybe there really *was* some deity from another dimension involved, trying to get into ours. I'd just seen someone's blood and the water go to pitch-black before my eyes. At that point, I was convinced it was all real. I figured that maybe if Rojachar had already been here, my brother would still be alive today. It all made sense. It was like a light bulb was turned on in my head."

"I don't understand," I say, confused

"I thought I could make the world a better place," she says, looking at me calmly. "Call it revenge, I don't know. When I saw the life leave Ridgehill's eyes, it felt *good*. It felt like this huge weight being lifted off my shoulders. I could sleep easier at night, knowing the man who did that my brother wouldn't be able to do it to anyone else again. After the body was taken away, Devin held his hand out to me. I looked up at him and took it. I got up, and he guided me to the center of the circle. He looked me deep in my eyes and told me to make sure to keep my eyes open while I was underwater. Then he slowly dunked me into the pool."

"What did you see?"

"Picture yourself lying on your back looking up into the night sky; that's what I saw at first. It was beautiful. It felt like I was having an out-of-body experience. Then it felt like I was floating up towards the stars. I could see and feel myself leaving the ground. Soon I was up in space with the stars. I was traveling through our solar system, leaving it behind. I felt so at peace. It was like nothing I never felt before or since. As I traveled, I knew I was leaving this universe, this dimension, or whatever you want to call it. I was in space still, but not our space. I saw this planet in the distance that looked like Earth. The closer I got to it, the more I felt this sense of dread, anxiety, depression, anger, and every other negative feeling there is. When I was a stone's throw away from the planet, I broke down in tears and cried like a baby. I could feel the negativity of the planet. I could feel all the corruption, evil, and heartache," she says as a few tears ran down her face. She reaches over and grabs a tissue to wipe them away.

"In the distance, I could see something like a thick, green cloud making its way towards the planet. It started to slowly swallow the planet. Soon, there was just this green cloud enveloping the planet. I couldn't see the planet itself anymore. I felt nothing more from the planet, either; all the bad feelings were gone. Soon, the cloud started to fade away from the planet, and everything felt different."

"Different how?"

"I couldn't feel the negativity that I'd felt before the cloud came. All I felt was peace, like everything was right with the world. At the same time, I felt something like a collective consciousness coming online. It's hard to explain. It was like everyone had the exact same train of thought. I know this sounds like some crazy drug trip, but I'm telling you the truth about everything I saw."

When she falls silent, I ask, "Then what?"

"Devin lifted me up from under the water. I know only a few seconds had passed in our world, but for me, during my vision, it felt like hours. I wiped the water from my eyes, and it was like suddenly

I understood everything. My purpose in life. I felt reborn."

Chapter 16

I walk back into the living room with a glass of water for Rachel. "Here you go," I say, handing it to her.

She smiles. "Thank you." She takes a few sips from the glass.

I sit down in my chair next to the camera. "What are you planning to do after you're done here?" I ask her quietly. "What I mean is, you have a wealthy cult most likely hunting you down. When I edit the video, I can blur your face and change your voice, and of course we'll use a false name, but that's about it."

She took another sip of her water and shrugged. "I'm going to London. My uncle lives there. He's giving me a job and letting me stay at his place till I get on my feet."

"Didn't you say the cult is active in Europe?

"Yes, but they're not as active as they are here in the States."

"So you have to go all way the other side of the world, pretty much, to escape the cult. And even then, you're in danger. I'm still surprised that the cult is global." I take a deep breath. "Are you ready to continue?"

She nods. "Ready when you are."

Once everything is ready to go, I press *Record* and point at her, letting her know the camera is recording. She nods. I lean back in my chair, looking at her. "You were in the cult for three years," I say. "Tell us what it was like."

"When you first join the cult, you do so at the rank of Acolyte. Like I said earlier, think of it as being a private in the army. You're given the jobs no one else wants to do. At first, it was nothing extreme. Working extra hours at work and not having the option to refuse. Running errands for the celebrities. Other stuff like that. As time went on, I started doing more cult activities. Some of that stuff included cleaning up after ceremonies, including disposing of... remains." Her voice cracked a little. "I got used to it. They trusted me and promoted me to Acolyte Supreme, and then moved me out to LA."

"What happened from there?"

"I had seven Acolytes working under me, and they assigned us all to a guy named Chad Parker, this big-time social media influencer and vlogger who has over 20 million people following his vlogs. We were his entourage, bodyguards, servants, pimps, whores, you name it. If he wanted drugs, we would get them. If he wanted women, we would get them. If he wanted us, he got us. Mostly, things were normal, if deviant sometimes... but then things got evil."

"Evil how?"

"People in California go missing a lot; it's nothing new. He would invite women over. Kill them, drain the blood from the bodies, and bathe in it. It was even better for him if they were virgins. He would justify it by saying he needed to stay youthful for Rojachar, so he could continue to use his celebrity status to have people join the cult. The acolytes and I would clean his mess up and get r-rid of the bodies. It was ingrained in our heads that with celebrities, you don't talk back, step out of line, or give an opinion. If you step out of line in any shape, form, or fashion, you're dealt with harshly. They have that luxury because the celebrities bring in a lot of members and make very large donations to the cult." She sighs sadly, looking down to the ground. "They were innocent women. Fans who just wanted to meet a celebrity. I'll give Devin this—he put an end to all of Chad's crap when he learned of it."

"How so?" I ask, intrigued.

"A girl went missing. Witnesses outside the cult said she was last seen with Chad. Police got involved. There was evidence pointing at Chad, suggesting that he had something to do with her disappearance. Then one day, poof. All that evidence just disappears. Devin made a few phone calls and paid off a few people. Devin was very upset that he had shell out large amounts of cash to fix Chad's mess, do Devin convinced him — and I use that term loosely — to make large donations to Highmore Entertainment, and also stop inviting people over to his place. We were no longer his entourage. We were his babysitters, for lack of a better term, to make sure he stayed out of trouble."

"Does the name Tiffany Natts ring a bell?" I ask her.

She nod wearily. "Yes, of course it does. I've seen the news broadcasts about her. She's not missing; she's safe and sound. She wasn't kidnapped or anything. She joined the cult willingly. She's the

Void Mother. No idea where she is, though. Only Devin and a few of the Enlightened know that."

"I keep hearing that 'Void Mother' thing. Just what *is* the Void Mother? What's Tiffany's role in all of this?"

"Rojachar will supposedly come to Earth through Tiffany. I'm not sure how she will give birth to a cosmic deity. All I know for sure is that Devin is planning something big for it. Once Rojachar is born, that's when the countdown begins."

"Countdown?" I asked.

"Yeah. When the child reaches 20, his powers will have matured; and when he dies on his 20th birthday, he will manifest in his true form. From there he'll swallow the world whole."

I press her. "And then what?"

"The world will be covered in darkness, whereupon his will, desires, and everything else will infect the mind of every thinking being on Earth. Humanity, and maybe a few of the more intelligent animal species, will become one giant hive-mind, and Rojachar will be the one in control. Afterwards, he'll leave Earth and go on to repeat the process across the universe, taking it over planet by inhabited planet. And yes, there *will* be peace — but there will be no free will."

"How did you find out about all this?" I ask her.

She shrugs. "Kim told me. When she did, I told her we had to leave the Order. When I first joined, I thought we would do something the law couldn't — provide justice for people who didn't get it. I felt good. It felt right to me. But I gradually came to realize, who am I to play judge, jury, and executioner?" She pauses for a moment, then grabs a tissue and wipes away a tear. "I wish I had tried harder to get her come with me."

I hand her a few more tissues. "Take your time. Would you like to take a break?"

She grabs the tissues and wipes the tears away. She takes a deep breath. "No, I'm fine. Let's keep going.

"When I confronted Kim about it, she told me I was overreacting, and kept brushing it off whenever I brought it up to her. A few days after I told Kim how I felt, members of the cult started following me all over the place. It started small, like bumping into them at the grocery store. Then it moved up to them tailing me around town and just watching me. I knew I had to escape. So I got my things together, and here I am now."

I take a deep breath. "How can all of this be stopped?" I ask her.

Her mouth twists, and she says, "Kill Tiffany before she gives birth. Or kill Rojachar while he's on Earth as a child, before he turns 20. Devin and the cult need to be stopped at all costs if humanity is to survive."

"Thank you for your time," I say gently. I get up and turned the camera off. "Great work, Natalie, but do you think this will help bring down the cult?" I take the camera off the tripod and walk over to my computer, then plug it in via a USB cord and start downloading the video onto my computer. "Devin can just claim this is all slander, and have my video taken down."

"At the very least, it'll get people talking," she said. "Maybe people who are already in the cult will leave. Maybe people will start looking at Tiffany's disappearance again."

"Once everything downloads, I'll start doing my edits. Give me some time, and I'll have this posted ASAP," I tell her. "I take it you're off to the airport now?"

She nods. "Yeah, I have my passport and my entire life in my backpack. Not looking forward to the long flight, but I'm going first class. So while I wait to get on the plane, I'll have some whiskey at the airport bar to calm my nerves, and later take something just so I can sleep the entire flight."

"Not a fan of flying?" I ask.

She shakes head. "Not a fan of being high in the air like that. I have a fear of heights. What about you?"

"What do you mean, what about me?"

"What are you going to do once the video is posted? They won't like this. I mean, once you post this, they won't stop coming after you," she said, grabbing her backpack and walking towards the door.

"I'll figure something out," I say, as I walk with her. "Hey, one last thing before you go." I grab my cell phone and show her a picture of Bret. "His name was Bret Pearsmith. Does he look familiar at all?"

She takes the phone and looks at it, then nods before returning it to me. "Yes, he was doing some research on the cult. Trying to bring everything to the light like you are. Devin found out and had him dealt with before that could happen. Did you know him?"

I nod. "He was a good friend. He's the reason I'm doing all this."

She gasps in shock, placing her hands over mouth, then gives me a quick hug. "Oh, I'm so sorry for your loss!"

"It's okay, You had no idea we were friends. I don't understand something, though. I'm posting videos, lots of them, and I'm still alive. They killed him before he even went public. How did they find out he was even planning to go public?"

She shakes her head, looking just as dumbfounded as I am. "I don't know what makes you different from Bret. I wish I could tell you, but I can't. I don't have the slightest idea."

We hug each other once more. "Take care of yourself," she tells me. "After your video is posted, you're gonna have a bullseye on your chest."

"Thank you. I'll keep my eyes open. One last thing before you go. " I walk over to my desk and grab a piece of paper. I write down my phone number and email, then walk back over and hand the paper to her. "My contact info. Let me know when you get to London."

She smiles and takes the paper, then takes out her cellphone and saves my contact info on her phone. "Okay. I sent you a text, so now you have my number." We hug one more time before she leaves. Once she's gone, I lock the door and give my government handlers a call about the interview.

"Yeah, she was in the cult," I reply to their barrage of questions. "We did an interview where she talked about what happened while she was there. No, I haven't posted it yet. I need to edit it. The raw footage? Yeah, go ahead and come by, and I'll have it ready for you two. Okay, I'll see you soon." I hang up the phone and open the drawer of my computer desk to dig around for a spare thumb drive. I find one, plug it into my computer, and start copying the video files.

About an hour goes by. I'm deep into my edit when my doorbell app alerts me that someone's at my door; this is followed by a knock. When I look at my phone, I see that it's the two USSSA agents. "Yeah, just a minute," I call. I make my way over to the door, thumb drive in hand. Once there, I unlock and open the door.

"How you doing, Jeffery?" Miller drawls.

"As well as I can in this situation."

"Do you have the footage?"

I hold out the thumb drive with the raw video on it. "Sure. Here you go."

He takes the thumb drive. "Thanks. Give us some time to look at the footage before you post the video. We'll give you a call to let you know when."

"They know where I live," I tell them.

Neither of them seems surprised. "We'll have some local cops sit outside the apartment complex. If something happens, help is just a few feet away," Hayes tells me, with no worry in her voice.

My eyes go wide at her lack of concern. "That's it?"

"They know where you are. If they wanted to do something, they would have done it by now. Just stay alert, and if something else comes up, call us."

"Gee, thanks." I reply, but my sarcasm is lost on them. I close the door as the two agents turn to leave. Jerks.

Chapter 17

It's been a friggin' day since the agents came by to get the raw video footage. I haven't left my apartment. I have the video edited and ready to go, and I'm waiting anxiously for word that I can post. Finally, my cell phone rings. USSSA calling. "Hello Jeffery, this is Agent Hayes. Agent Miller and I looked at your footage. This information will help with the investigation, but there's a problem."

"What's the problem?" I ask, irritated.

"The stuff about Tiffany Natts — remove it from the final version. We feel it would be in the best interests of the investigation for you not to post it."

"You're joking, right? This just isn't some random conspiracy theorist. The girl was part of—"

Before I can finish, Hayes cuts me off mid-sentence. "Jeffery, I understand your passion to bring this cult to justice, but if you leave in the footage regarding Tiffany Natts, then things will become *very* problematic. If you mention that a woman who's been missing for a year is being held captive by the owner of very large,

148

very wealthy entertainment agency, it will attract too much unwanted attention by police, media, her family, the cult, and everyone in between. You'll be brought in for questioning by the police and could see prison time — and if you are, we won't help you out like we did in LA."

"I'll post it anyway. People need to know about this, about Tiffany. Will the video get taken down? Most likely, but only after everyone who follows me sees it. That's the power of social media. You guys need me, considering this is the closest you've gotten to the cult," I tell Hayes arrogantly, thinking I have her on the ropes.

"It's social media that makes you replaceable, Jeffery," she snaps. "When people see your video they'll do their own research, maybe even find out stuff you haven't yet. Some will want to act against the cult. That's when we'll find another content creator who will abide by our rules of engagement. Do we want you? Yes. Do we absolutely need you? No. Stop and think, Jeffery. Do only what you want, and this will not end well for you. We *will* shut down your accounts, cutting off your main source of income and, if need be, we will make disappear. These are not threats. These are guarantees. Do what you're told, and you'll be compensated. Disobey, and you'll be punished."

Her threat hits me like a punch to the gut. She's right about everything. If I don't do what I'm told, I know they'll just find someone else who will follow their lead without pushback. I couldn't live with myself — assuming I lived — knowing I could have contributed to bringing down this murderous cult. Reluctantly, I tell her I'll edit the bit about Tiffany out. She thanks me and hangs up.

Chapter 18

It's 5 PM, and it's been about an hour since I posted the video. Traffic is high and the comments on the video have grown like a wildfire. There's been a mixture of all types of comments. Some think this is just some desperate ploy to increase my popularity. Some think it's part of a horror series I'm inventing, and that I got Devin's okay to mention him. A few even believe me. My email inbox is flooded emails trying to get a straight answer out of me.

My phone rings, and the Caller ID reads "Donnie." Donnie Alp and I work together every now and then. His content is mostly video-game related. I answer, and before I can even say hello, he starts talking. "What the hell are doing!? What's with that video you posted!?" he shouts at me, demanding answers.

"It's the truth," I reply calmly.

"You're saying *Devin Fucking Highmore* is the leader of a deadly cult by night and owner of a major entertainment agency by day? Seriously? Look, I'm all for getting more views, but you can't go around posting stuff like this! This is libel material, and it could get your account terminated!" He sounds like he's panicking.

"Thank you for your concerns, Donnie," I say coolly, "but I understand what I'm getting myself into. Everything's going to be fine."

"Really? Well, Highmore Entertainment just issued a press release saying they like your very creative series, but nothing like that is happening there."

"Look, this isn't something I came up with to get more followers!" I exclaimed. "All of this is *real.* I know I sound batshit insane, but you gotta trust me on this!"

"Listen to yourself, man. You sound fucking crazy. When's the last time you got any sleep?"

"My sleep has been all over the place, thanks. Been too busy trying to figure all this out and bring this cult down and into the light. You ever heard of Tiffany Natts? She's a girl who went missing about a year and a half ago. Highmore Entertainment has her."

"Thank you for proving my point. You need to get some sleep. I get it; you want to produce good content..."

Before he can finish his sentence, I hang up, frustrated that he doesn't believe me. I pace back and forth in the living room, thinking about everything I've learned, and everything I still haven't. I walk over to my computer and print out all the info I've gathered thus far on the cult. I lay out stacks of paper on my coffee table, so I have an improved view of it all. I pin a printout of Devin's picture on the wall. Next to his picture, I pin some information about Highmore Entertainment. Below his picture are pictures of famous content creators, actors, and other entertainers who work for Highmore Entertainment.

Next, I hang up a picture of Tiffany Natts. Beside her picture, I hang a picture of a person who has been ruled out as being be Tiffany Natts. She was last seen in Burnsley, Washington. The woman in the picture has short black hair, as opposed to Tiffany's blonde hair. The woman in the picture also appears to be pregnant. The sighting was at a gas station about three months ago. I take a closer look at the picture of Tiffany and the blacked-hair woman;

there's a chance the latter *could* be Tiffany. They look similar, but at the same time, it might *not* be her. I look up the phone number for the gas station and give it call.

It rings a few times before someone on the other end picks up. "Kenny's Gas and Go. This is Mark, how can I help you?"

"Hi Mark, my name is Carl Hill. I'm with the FBI, working with the family of a missing girl named Tiffany Natts. I have a few questions."

"Sure, go ahead and ask," he replies, sounding doubtful. "I don't know how much help I would be, though."

"Thank you. I'll get right to the point. I'm with a task force trying to bring Tiffany home from a cult. About three months ago, a woman resembling Tiffany came into the gas station you work at. The local authorities believed it was her, but after further investigation, they decided it wasn't," I explain.

"Yeah, I heard about the missing girl. I was there that day when she came in with her friends. Two guys were outside filling up their car, and she was in here with a woman getting some snacks and other stuff, nothing major. When she was paying for her stuff, she talked about how her son was going change the world for the better. I didn't think it was a big deal, just a proud soon-to-be mom."

His words send a charge through me. "Did anything stand out at all? Even the smallest detail?" I asked, hoping that he would give me something more to work with.

"No, sorry, it was normal. They got gas and snacks and left. Oh, wait... there *was* something a little weird. They all wore matching outfits that were kind of odd, but not a big deal."

"What do you mean, matching outfits? "

"Well, everyone but the pregnant woman had on green tops. Like dress-shirt tops."

I feel like a light has just turned on in my head. I'm thinking that it had to have been Tiffany. "Hmm, interesting. Thank you so much for your help, Mark."

When I hang up the phone, I immediately call Agents Miller and Hayes. When Miller answers, I immediately start speaking before he can get a single word out. "I need your help," I begin.

157

Chapter 19

A day has passed since I called asking the USSSA agents for help. We had talked briefly about what I'd learned, and then decided the three of us would fly out to Burnsley. They arranged it quickly, and when we arrived, we rented a one-bedroom apartment that we would use as a base of operations. The living room is our work area. Scattered on the floor are stacks of folders filled with files pertaining to the investigation. The three of us sit at a folding table with a laptop in front of each of us. "So, you're sure this girl is Tiffany after all?" Miller asks.

"Positive. She was with people who looked like the cult, green tops and all. The girl was pregnant, too. I'm no doctor, but if had to guess, I'd say her due date is coming up real soon."

"So, we just have to find one pregnant girl in a town of more than 60,000 people. All we have is a picture. The gas station camera wasn't at a good angle to get a view of the license plate. Any idea how we'll find her?" Miller asked.

Hayes smiled. "Old fashioned detective work. We have the fact that she's pregnant going for us. Tiffany still has to go to the doctor to make sure her pregnancy is going well."

"There are some huge holes in your logic, Hayes. Devin wouldn't have her using her real name. Plus, he's rich enough to have a doctor make house calls, so she surely isn't out in public much, if ever. And even if she has a doctor, there's the issue of doctor-patient confidentiality," Miller comments dryly.

As they talk, I search for doctors that Tiffany would most likely visit. "Okay, there are 80 medical facilities she could go to. Maybe the local police would have some info? They're the ones who cleared her."

Miller shake his head. "Too risky. This cult has a lot of power, so it wouldn't surprise me if the local police are on Highmore Entertainment's payroll. We need to remain under the radar as much as possible. You definitely need to stay here and keep out of sight.

159

Run support here. The only reason we brought you here is for your own safety. I prefer that we keep an eye on you rather than someone else."

"I didn't know you cared," I reply sarcastically.

"I don't," he states coldly. "You're a tool, nothing more."

I roll my eyes. "So, what's the plan? We can't just go to each facility. That would take way too long."

"What about the news station?" Hayes suggested. "They released the information about the girl. The cops had to have talked to them before they did. At the very least, the cops told the station not to release anything about her being Tiffany. It's a long shot, and if it doesn't work, we'll start questioning the doctor's offices then."

Miller nods. "Better than nothing. I'll look up the address for the station."

I stand up from the table and start getting ready. "All right, let's go."

Miller looks at me, confused. "Where are you going?"

"I'm going with you two."

Miller shakes his head quickly, with an expression that says, *Hell no, no way that's not happening.* I continue to get ready, ignoring his disapproval. "You said yourself," I point to him and Hayes, "that you brought me here to keep an eye on me. What better way to keep an eye on than for me to go with you?"

Hayes glances at Miller. "He has a point. If the cult's here in town, the three of us need to be stay together for his safety."

Miller looks at both of us, then sighs in defeat. "Fine. If anyone asks, you're an intern."

The three of us drive to the television station in silence. As I sat there in the car, I just stare at the people in town around us, carrying on with the lives. I wonder if any of them are members of the cult. I look for green shirts. I wonder if they already know we're here. They probably will after we check in at the TV station.

"You think they know we're here yet?" I asked the agents from the back seat.

"It's possible," Hayes replies.

"And if they do?"

"We'll cross that bridge when we come to it, kid. For now, let's just focus on finding the girl," Miller growls from the driver's seat.

The town is fairly small, so it doesn't take us long to get to the three-story building housing KXBC. The stations' lobby is a busy one, filled with people coming and going, tending to whatever tasks they need to accomplish as if they're critical to the survival of the free world. To the right is a large reception desk, with two women behind it who look to be in their mid-20s. We walk over to the desk, where Miller and Hayes wave their badges at the receptionists. "I'm Agent Miller. This is Special Agent Hayes, and he's our intern, William. We're with the U.S. Special Security Agency."

"How can we help you today?" one of the young ladies asks, eyes wide.

Hayes reaches into her inner suit jacket pocket and holds out the picture of Tiffany from the gas station. "A while ago, your news station did a broadcast about how this girl was mistaken for a missing girl named Tiffany Natts." She lays down a picture of Tiffany before she went missing, and adds the picture of Tiffany down with black hair. "We heard about this so-called mistaken identity, and we're following up on it."

The receptionist leans in and takes a closer look at both pictures. She turns her attention back to us and shakes her head, frowning. "It's a shame they still haven't found Tiffany. I was a fan of her vlogs, you know? I don't know anything about the girl with the black hair, though. I could call the producer down. The police talked to him the most about everything involving that."

Hayes smiles, an expression I've never seen on her before, and says sweetly, "Thank you, that will be very helpful." Who knew she could be so pleasant? The woman deserves an Oscar.

The receptionist smiles back, then picks up the phone and presses a few buttons on the keypad. "Hi, Mr. Bradford. I have some people from the government here in the lobby, wanting to speak to you about the girl everyone thought was Tiffany Natts. Uh-huh, okay, thank you." She points at a sitting area. "Please have a seat. Mr. Bradford will be down soon. There's coffee over there if you want some. All kinds of pods for the Keurig. Give the French Vanilla a try. That one is my favorite."

Miller smiles and nods. "Thank you," he says warmly. Another Oscar-worthy performance! We walk over to the sitting area she pointed out. Hayes takes a seat, while Miller and I take advantage of the free coffee. I like the French Vanilla.

"How long have you two been working together?" I ask Miller at the Keurig. I figure I should at least try to get to know something about my government babysitters.

"Three years," he answers as he places a white Styrofoam cup under the dispenser part of the coffee machine. He also takes the receptionist's advice and tries a French Vanilla coffee pod. Once the machine finishes pouring the coffee, he grabs the cup and sips on the coffee, not adding anything to it. I shuddered a bit at the fact he's drinking it black. Mine is loaded with sugar and cream.

"What's your plan after this case?" I ask him as we both walk over to where Hayes wait and sit.

Miller takes another sip of his coffee, then glances at me. "Look, we aren't friends or anything. We have a common interest. and that's bringing down this cult. You do what you need to do.

You'll get paid and you can go back to your pretend job of making Internet videos."

His comment about my vlogging being a "pretend job" strikes a nerve. "Look, believe it or not, my videos make me money. My *pretend job* pays my bills, which pretty much makes it a real job," I tell him angrily. "It's not just a hobby. People have become millionaires doing what I do, started their own business, have their own merchandise."

"Okay, let me ask you this. Do you have a retirement plan? Benefits? What happens when the next big thing comes along?" he asks arrogantly, as if he has all the answers.

"Look, I'm working on all that stuff. It just takes time. Rome wasn't built in a day." I look at Hayes. "You agree with me, right? These things take time." I ask, hoping she'll take my side as she did back at the apartment. I notice she has a blank, far-off stare on her face. "Uh, hello? Earth to Agent Hayes."

Hayes breaks her blank stare, and looks at Miller and I. "I'm sorry, I don't have an opinion on the subject. I don't spend time on the Internet unless it's work related."

"What do you do in your free time, then?" I ask.

"I have very little free time."

Miller points to a portly man in a chocolate-brown suit talking to the receptionist. "That must be him."

The receptionist points us out, and the man walks over to us with a large smile on his face. "Hello, gentlemen and lady, Charles Bradford." He offers his hand to us. The three of us stand, and we each shake his hand and introduce ourselves.

"Thank you for taking the time to see us," Miller says brightly. "Is there a place we can talk in private?"

Bradford smiles and nods. "Sure. Let's head upstairs to my office. Please follow me."

We thank him and follow him to an elevator, which whisks us up to the top floor. His office is large and elegant. Displayed on the walls are awards that he and the station have achieved over the years. He takes a seat behind his large desk and we sit down across from him. "The receptionist told me why you're here. It's a shame that the missing girl hasn't been found yet. I have two girls myself,

15 and 10, and I wouldn't know what to do if one of them went missing."

"Yes, this is a terrible situation, Mr. Bradford—"

Miller gets cut off by the man. "Please, call me Charles. My father is Mr. Bradford," he says in an upbeat tone.

Miller nods and smiles. "Charles, seeing as how your receptionist brought you up to speed, I'll cut to the case. We need any information that the police may have given you that wasn't made known to the public."

"Such as?" Charles asks.

"Anything would be helpful. For starters, do you have the name of the woman mistaken as Tiffany Natts?" I ask. Miller gives me a glare, as if to say, *Shut up and let me handle this.*

"I do, but I can't give you that information," Charles says in a hesitant tone.

"You can or you won't?" Miller asks.

"Okay, I won't. There's this thing called journalistic integrity."

167

"*Journalistic integrity!?*" I yell, standing straight up as my chair falls back and I slam my hands on his desk. "A girl is missing, and you won't help us out because of *journalistic integrity!?* You have kids! What if one of your girls was missing?"

Charles glares and says, "Yes, I have kids. At the same time, this job supports my family. If I were to give you information that I promised I wouldn't share, I would most likely lose my job if someone found out. Unless you have some piece of paper signed by a judge saying I *must* give you this information, which I don't think you do, then this meeting is over."

"Take a seat, intern," Miller demands.

I ignore him as I stare daggers at the smug producer. "I'm not asking, *Charles*. I'm *demanding* you give us all the information you have," I say in a calm yet forceful tone, clenching my fists in anger.

Charles shakes his head. "No. Now if you'll excuse me, I have other meetings to attend to today." He waves his hands in a shooing motion, like we're stray dogs.

"Not until you give us something," I demand once more.

"That's it. I'm calling security." He reaches for the phone on his desk, and as he does, my eyes widen in panic. I know he's the key to finding Tiffany, and I didn't come this far to get turned away. My eyes dart over to a pair of scissors on the desk. I grab them with one hand, and with my other I grab his necktie. With all my strength and anger, I almost yank him across the desk. I hold the tip of the scissors against the side of his neck. "I am very, very close to my breaking point," I inform him in a low voice. "You have *no idea* what I have been through to get this far. Now *tell me what you know*."

His breathing deepens, and beads of nervous sweat run down his forehead. "You're just going to let him do this?! You work for the government!" he cries, looking at Miller and Hayes, panicking. They say nothing. Hayes just looks on, while Miller take out his phone and starts messing with it. "Are you fucking *kidding* me?" the producer yells.

I pierce his skin slightly, just enough to draw a bit of blood. "Tell me what you know!" I demanded once more.

"Becky, Becky Wilson! That's the girl that everyone got confused with Tiffany Natts!" he answers in a panicked tone.

"Where does she live?" I asked still holding the scissors.

"I don't know, I don't know!" he replied in the same panicked toned.

As soon as the words *I don't know* escape his lips, I know he's lying. Something inside me snaps. I quickly stabbed the scissors directly in the center of his hand left hand, which is splayed out on the desk. *"Where is she!?"* I scream.

The two agents jump up from their seats and pull me off him. With his hand still stuck to the desk via the scissors, Charles falls to his knees, crying out in pain, "3545 West Green Lane! Two-story red brick house out in the countryside away from everyone else! They invited me there for dinner, and paid me to make sure her name wouldn't get out into the public! I promise that's all I know!"

I reach over and pull the scissors out of his hand, and he falls to the carpet, doubled over, holding his hand and moaning in pain.

The two agents usher me out of the office and the building. They push me into the car and quickly drive off the property, heading back to the apartment. "What the hell was that back there?" Miller demands.

I take a deep breath to calm myself, as adrenaline still courses through my body. "I call it 'effective questioning.' I'm sorry, but he had the information we needed, and he wasn't talking."

"Granted, your method of obtaining the information was effective, but there's a high possibility that he'll let the cult know that we're here in town looking for them." Hayes snaps.

Miller keeps speeding down the street. It doesn't take us long to get back to the apartment. "So, let's go grab her," I say as we walked into the apartment.

"Shut up! Shut the fuck up!" Miller turns to me. "It's because of you that all this may be for nothing, and may put us back at Square One! This whole operation may be compromised now!" He reaches for his phone and swipes and tap the screen. "But you're right, we need to grab her now."

Once he's done roaring at me in anger, he walks away with his phone to his ear. "Authentication number 66420. Last name Miller, first name Kenneth. I need a mobile task force unit immediately." He shakes his head. "Not soon enough; I need something now. Okay, that works. Trace the location of my cell and send it to the MTF. In the meantime, I'll send over everything they need to know to the task force leader so he can brief his team."

Miller hangs up, walks over to his laptop, and starts to furiously type and click. I notice an odd-looking using interface pop up on his laptop. On-screen are the letters AIA. Inside, I begin to panic once more. *They aren't government agents*, I immediately think. I walk over to the files, pretending that I need to look at them. As I walk over, I quickly push Hayes down to ground, catching her off guard. As I push her, I reach for her gun. I'm able to grab it from her holster and aim it at both of them. Noticing this, Miller quickly gets up, drawing his own gun and aiming it at me. Hayes rises, glaring at both of us.

"Put the gun down, Jeffery!" Miller yells at me.

"Fuck you! Who the hell are you two? What's AIA?" I yell.

"We are United States Special Security, Jeffery," Hayes answers calmly.

"Screw you, you're not with the government! No one has given me a straight answer since all this started. I'm going to ask you one more time! Tell me who you are, or I'm shooting!"

"You know what? Fuck you, vlogger! You have been nothing but one giant pain in the ass from Day One! Hayes, I'm going to put two right between his eyes and call a cleanup crew!"

Hayes steps between Miller and I. She places her hands on the ends of our guns and slowly pushes them down. She then turns around and directs all her attention to me. "You're right, Jeffery... kind of. We *are* with the government, but we're not with a group called Special Security. There is no such thing; we just use that as a cover for when we go out in the public."

I quickly lift the gun back up, this time pointing it at her. "Yeah, no shit, I can tell! So who the hell are you two?"

Hayes looks at me, trying to be the voice of reason of the three of us. "We're with an organization called the Abnormal Investigation Agency, or AIA. We specialize in matters that other law enforcement agencies are not equipped to handle. Matters that

deal with the occult, the paranormal, and other things of that
nature."

"Why didn't you tell me all this in the first place?" I ask.
"Wouldn't it have made things a lot easier?"

Miller shrugs. "We doubted that. When we first noticed your
videos, we started to monitor you. Watching your Internet history.
Listening in on your phone calls. We needed to rule out the
possibility that you were part of the cult, and in time, we concluded
that you weren't. When we found out you were heading to LA, we
went as well. When the local police took you into custody, we
needed to you get you out. We got you out so we could, to put it
bluntly, use you for our gain."

"Fuck you! You used me for bait! You got my friend
kidnapped in LA and forced into a cult! His friends died, all because
of you two!" I yelled, lifting the gun back up and aiming it at them,
shaking with fury.

"You're damn right! And you know what? I'd do it again!"
Miller snarls. "Your friends weren't our priority, *you* were! Now put
the gun down, or I will pop two between your eyes!"

I stand there, not staying anything, still shaking in anger, the gun aimed at Miller. My finger is on the trigger, ready to shoot him dead.

Miller stands there as a smirk creeps onto his face. "Look at you. You've never killed anyone. Closet thing was someone you killed in one of your video games. You're not a killer, Jeffery. You don't know how to kill. You've never had to wash another person's blood off your hands. Dig it out from under your fingernails." Miller suddenly holsters his gun, and opens his arms. "Let's go, killer! Hayes, get out the way. Our Jeffery is about to go from vlogger to killer with a pull of a trigger. Get your phone out and record it, Hayes, so you can post it on his vlog."

"Fuck you!" I yell, raising the gun to his center mass.

"Here, let me easier for you!" Miller grabs a red marker from my coffee table and draws a giant X on the center of his forehead. "There you go. Shoot the X!"

I raise the gun, my hands stead now, thinking about how it would be so easy to shoot him right in the head, and not have to put up with his shit anymore. Unfortunately, he's right. I'm not a killer.

Even if I were, I'd go to jail for life for killing him, no matter how much he provoked me. So I lower the gun and put a bullet into the carpet between his legs, missing his groin by inches at best. Then I calmly hand the gun off to Hayes and storm up to him, barely noticing the dark stain in his crotch where he pissed his pants when I called his bluff. That only registers later.

I look Miller dead in the eyes, still wondering and wishing I'd put a bullet between them before I handed Hayes back her gun. "Fuck you," I spit at him. "Do you need me? No, apparently not. Your partner made that clear the other day. But she was full of shit. So let's clear the air. Right now, I'm all that you have. Something happens to me, you guys really are back to Square One. So do me a favor: treat me with *some fucking respect!*" I scream the last few words at him.

Miller just looks me the same rage at first; but it slowly fades, and a grin creeps across his face. "Well, you got a pair after all. Relax, Jeffery. Grab a beer from the fridge." Miller walks by me, sits down, and goes back to typing on the laptop. "I'm finishing up this mission briefing to send to the mobile task force. If everything goes well, before the sun rises tomorrow, we'll have Tiffany in custody and we can question her."

"Do you really believe that she's about to give birth to this god that they worship?" I ask him.

Miller types furiously, switching his gaze from the laptop screen to files on the table. "It wouldn't surprise me. We've dealt with things far beyond the realm of 'normal' before."

"Seriously? Like what?"

Hayes chimes in with, "Classified."

I rolled my eyes. "Sure, why did I even ask? Anyway, shouldn't we be meeting up with this mobile task force?"

Miller shakes his head. "No, we'd just get in their way. AIA mobile task forces consist of former military, SWAT, Special Forces, the like. Best of the best. They'll provide us with a live feed, and we'll run the show from here while they do what they need to do. For now, just kick back till they get back to us, all right, kid?"

Chapter 20

The three of us sit in front of the laptop. Miller is in the middle while I'm on the left, with Hayes on the right. Exactly one hour after submitting his report, Miller's phone starts ringing. He immediately picks up. "This is Miller. Yeah, I'm logging in, now thanks." With a few keystrokes, a live feed comes up. In the center of the screen is one large live feed; and on the left side of the screen are five smaller feeds. All six feeds display a large two-story house that fits the description that the producer, Charles, gave us of where Tiffany is now. On the left-hand corner of each live feed is the name and rank of each person associated with each feed. "Sergeant Anders, can you hear me?" Miller asks.

A voice comes from the laptop speakers. "This is Anders; I read you five-by-five. We have eyes on the house. It's out in the middle of nowhere, just like you said. That works for us, because we don't have to worry about civilians outside the containment area. I have another team working on cutting power to the house. Once the power is cut, both teams will move in and extract the target. My team will take the front while the other takes the back."

"Perfect. Sorry for the lack of details on how many people could be in there." Miller gives me a side-eye glare, then turns his attention back to the laptop. "We had unforeseen circumstances come up."

"Don't worry about it. My team and I are used to the unexpected. Just another mission for us," Anders said with confidence. "I read the mission briefing. To confirm: grab the pregnant girl and get out by any means?"

"Correct. Get in, grab the girl, and get out."

"Agent Miller, when I was reading the mission briefing, it said that a Summa-level entity is maturing inside her. I just want to make sure I read that correctly."

Hayes leans in close to the laptop. "Sergeant, this is Agent Hayes. Yes, you are correct."

Anders pauses before speaking again. "Okay, I just follow orders. We'll retrieve the target alive, and not a hair on her head will be out of place. Once the house goes dark, we'll move in. Stand by."

The three of us sit there waiting for the power to be cut, and I speak up. "He said 'Summa Level entity'. What does that mean? "

Her eyes focused on the screen, Hayes explains. "AIA has a threat level system. Going from less threatening to most you have Humilis, Mediestas, Altum. For rare cases, we have Summa."

"What makes this Summa?" I ask, also not looking away from the screen.

"We consider Summa-level beings and items world-ending," Hayes says in a tone that makes it seem not such a big deal.

I look at Hayes curiously. "You seem calm for something that could end the world."

"Kid, we deal with Summas once every couple of years, so this isn't new to us. Besides, it makes no sense to panic. If we panic, we won't be able to do our jobs effectively, and the world ends."

"If we capture her… "

Miller cuts me off. "*When* we capture her."

180

I look at Miller, then back at Hayes. "WHEN we capture her, what happens to her?"

"Not our place to decide; that's above our pay grade. All we're told is that they want her alive," Hayes responds.

I turned my attention back to the screen, wondering what the government would do to a woman and her Summa-level baby. Science experiments? Prison time? Death? Tiffany's baby could end the world. Would the government really kill a mother and her baby? Probably, if the stakes were truly that high.

While I sit there looking at the screen, wondering what might happen to this girl and her child, the mansion loses power. "Umbra One, Umbra Two. Power to the house is cut. Be advised, enemy personnel are armed," says a voice from the laptop speakers.

"Copy, Umbra Two. We will take the downstairs, while you handle the upstairs," Anders responds.

"Copy, Umbra One. You're up, we're down."

"Correct. Mission is a go. NV on," Anders says as we see his team moving towards the house. The feeds switch from near-darkness to green-hued night vision. Anders' team is equipped like a Special Forces black ops team... or at least, how I imagine such a team would be equipped. They proceed to the mansion like a well-oiled machine, maintaining a tight formation and keeping spoken communication at a minimum. I see Anders' hand make a series of gestures, ending with two fingers up. "Two hostiles at the door," Miller interprets. "Taking them out." Before he finishes speaking, two of Anders' team members lift their silenced assault rifles and, with a single pull of their triggers, the two guards at the door drop like sacks of potatoes, heads wrecked. I barely even hear the shots.

They reach the front door and three individuals line up on each side. Two individuals place what I guess are some small explosives on each corner of the door, then one in the center. I hear a double click on the channel. "Charges set," Miller says. Anders' hand is in view, his fingers counting down to a full fist; the door blasts off its hinges into the mansion, pieces of the door acting as improvised shrapnel. Weapons ready, crouching low, the team storms the mansion.

Four armed cult members stand in the mansion's foyer, and are instantly gunned down. Anders makes a series of gestures, which Miller translates in a monologue: "You three take left. You two come with me. Start clearing the mansion. Find the target and eliminate everyone else." On the laptop screen, I can see Anders and the two men with him head into the living room. They're met with two more armed cult members, who are put down with ease, and continue looking for Tiffany. The team that Anders told to go left is in the kitchen. No one's in the kitchen. "Kitchen clear!" one of them reports. Apparently, the time for silence is over.

They move from the kitchen and into the dining room, where they encounter two armed cult members and come under fire. As the Voiders fire, they take cover behind a nearby wall, as do the members from Umbra One on the other side of the room. "Contact, contact!" one member of Umbra Team One yells as a firefight ensues.

Anders and the two men with him come around to flank the cult members and shoot them behind, killing them. "Casualties?" Anders asks his men.

"We're good." Anders replies. Gunfire can be heard from upstairs, then a crisp voice on the radio. "Umbra One, Umbra Two. Upstairs is clear, but no sign of the package."

"Downstairs also clear. No sign of the package here either. Keep looking. Check for panic rooms. Stay frosty; there could be more of them," Anders cautions.

"Copy. Searching now."

The teams continue to search the mansion. My eyes are glued to the screen, hoping they find Tiffany. Ten minutes go by before both the upstairs and downstairs teams report that they can't locate anyone or anything.

I sigh in defeat. "The fucking producer must have told them we were coming."

"We'll head over there and check the mansion ourselves. See if we can find anything they missed," Miller said emotionlessly.

"Hold on, we may have found something," Anders says, looking at a door. "Looks like a safe room, possible a cellar." He turns the knob to open it, but it's locked. "Put a blast charge on it," Anders orders. One of the men does so, repeating the same process as the front door. The men take cover away from the blast. "Umbra Two, be advised we are blasting a door. Door blasting in 3, 2, 1, blasting." Just like the front door, they blow this door into pieces.

On the other side is a set of stairs going down. They men of Umbra Team One slowly and cautiously head down the stairs. Once downstairs, they find themselves in a large, open area converted into a makeshift office with two computers, some moving boxes, and a large map of an island. In one corner is the body of the friendly producer, Charles, with a single gunshot wound to the head. "No girl, but maybe this stuff here can help. Looks like they were in the middle of packing up."

"Grab the hard drives from the computers and the map and bring them here. I'm sending you my location now. Take everything else to the closest AIA facility and call in a cleaning crew. Great work, Sergeant."

"We should have it dropped off within the hour," Anders replies. "Umbra Team out." The laptop screen goes dark.

Chapter 21

The three of us sit there at the table, waiting for Anders to drop off everything he and his men recovered from the mansion. I break the silence at last. "Now we really are back at Square One. That fucking producer tipped them off! Who knows where she is?"

"Relax. We'll look at the hard drives and that map they found," Miller says, just as a loud pounding comes from the front door.

"Got it," Hayes says, getting up and drawing her gun. She peers through the peephole and cracks open the door just enough to grab a box. She closes the door, locks it tight, and walks over the table with a box. Inside are two hard drives and a folded map.

"I'll hang up the map," she says. "Miller, can you get the docking bay for the hard drives and see what's on them?"

Miller reaches into his bag and pulls out a docking bay for the hard drives, much to my surprise. He affixes the hard drives to the bay and goes to work checking them. Meanwhile, I help Hayes hang the map.

Once it's on the wall straight, I step back, looking at the map. It's the map of an island, with areas marked off for tents, bleachers, and makeshift restaurants; in the center of the island is a stage for performances. A legend on the bottom left-hand corner of the map reads *Cleo Marie Island.* "Cleo Marie Island," I mused. "I've heard of that place. Fancy houses there for rent. Rich people, celebrities, and spring breakers go there for a getaway to party and such. It's nothing special." I tell them.

"Well, it's something special to them. Come look," Miller says. Hayes and I walk over to Miller to look at what he has up on the screen. "Plans for suicide bombers to attend at three-day musical festival that Devin Highmore is planning. Calls it The Festival of a New Era."

I remembered what Natalie had said while Miller talked. "That's where it will happen. During my interview with the girl from the cult, she said that Devin has something major planned to bring Rojachar on to earth. They're planning to do a mass sacrifice." I grab my things and throw them into my bag. "Let's go; we can stop him right now. We know Highmore Entertainment's main office is in New York."

Hayes shakes her head. "Bad idea. Highmore knows we're on his trail now. Security is more than likely on high alert, and that plan will result in too much collateral damage. We'll end this at the festival. We can blend in with everyone else there."

Miller sits there tapping his fingers against the table, lost in thought. After a few seconds, he stops tapping. "I need to make a phone call."

Chapter 22

A man stands on the shore of a tropical beach, looking straight at a camera crew. He wears an emerald-green suit tailored perfectly to his body, and a matching dress shirt and tie. Not a single strand of his straight, jet-black shoulder-length hair with emerald green tips is out of place. The smile on his face stretches from ear to ear as he speaks.

"Hello, I'm Devin Highmore, owner and founder of Highmore Entertainment. At Highmore Entertainment, we're more than just a collection of actors, actresses, musicians, and Internet personalities. We are a family. Thanks to you, our family has grown. Thanks to you, Highmore Entertainment has given everyday people like you the chance to achieve their dreams. You're all part of our family.

"Since the announcement of The Festival of a New Era four months ago, everyone has been talking about it. Here on Cleo Marie Island, this is going to be more than just a three-day event where you can hang out with your fellow family members and have a few drinks, listen to remarkable live music, and meet members of Highmore Entertainment. Look at it as a creative retreat where anyone, regardless of age, race, sex, profession, and so on, can come together as one mind. One mind to start a new era, a new renaissance, a new age of peace."

Devin walks up to the camera and stares deeply at it. "I know I'll see you all there."

"Cut!" a man off camera yells.

"How was that?" Devin asks in an enthusiastic tone.

"Perfect, boss. We'll have this edited and have the video all over the Internet in a few hours. I don't care who I have to talk to, pay, kill, or whatever, I'll make sure that this is trending and all over social media. We'll have people from all over the globe coming to this event. The Great Void will be born, and then this world will truly know peace," the man says, clenching his fists, smiling widely.

"That's why you're my head of marketing, Kent. You know what we need, and you take it," Devin says.

A woman in an emerald green suit walks over to Devin; following behind her are three other men in green suits. "Ah, there she is, my head of security." Devin walks over to the girl with open arms and hugs her, then looks at her with a smile on his face. "Kim, how is everything?"

"Well, sir, very well," Kim replies.

"I heard what happened in Burnsley."

"Sir, let me assure you, it's taken care of. Tiffany is safe on the island," Kim says reassuringly.

"Walk with me, Kim. Bring your friends." Devin ambles down the shoreline. Kim glances at the other three men, and they all follow Devin. "Do you know what insurance is, Kim?" Devon asks after a moment.

Kim replies, "Of course, sir, but I'm not sure of the context you mean."

"You get sick, and insurance helps you pay for your treatment. You get in a car wreck, and insurance pays for the damage. You have a head of security, and they make sure the Mother of the Void is safe and that no one knows her whereabouts." He says

all this in a stern, angry tone.

"Yes, sir. I understand that, but Tiffany *is* safe," Kim replies

uncertainly.

"Burnsley shouldn't have happened in the first place!" Devin

yells, whirling to face her.

Kim takes a deep breath and responds, "Mr. Highmore, you

are correct. That is why I currently have everyone on high alert.

Tiffany has 24-hour security. I will make sure that the birth goes

perfectly. You have my word."

Devin smiles and open his arms to her. "Of course. I'm sorry,

Kim. I just want all this to go perfectly. We've been working toward

this time for generations, you know. We're bringing The Great Void

into this world. Soon, the world will know peace. Come here," he

says, smiling widely. They embrace lovingly. "It's okay, Kim, stuff

happens." Looking at the three men that accompanied them, Devin

points to one of the holstered guns on one man's hip. Devin opens

his hand, motioning for the gun to be placed in his hand. Without

hesitation, the man walks over Devin and places the gun in his hand.

"That's why we have insurance, Kim," Devin continues. He presses the gun up to Kim's temple. "I wish I could say you'll be one with The Great Void, but he, just like me, does not reward failure."

"NO, WAIT!" she screams. But before Kim can get another word out, Devin pulls the trigger. Blood, bone, and bits of brain matter spatter onto the sand. Devin releases Kim's lifeless body, letting it fall to the ground.

Devin holds the gun out to the man who first handed it to him. "Thank you."

The man walks over, taking and holstering the gun without saying a word.

Devin sighs. "Fun fact. This is only the second member of the Order I have had to kill. The first was the leader before me. He claimed to be the Voice of The Void. He was wrong, so I killed him. I will have nothing but perfection for The Great Void's arrival. Do I make myself clear?"

The three men nod vigorously, and the man whose gun was used to kill Kim bleats, "Yes, Mr. Highmore, you have made yourself *very* clear!"

Devin nods. "Perfect. Now, get rid of her body." He walks away, saying over his shoulder in a jovial tone, "We have a birthday party to plan, and it will be the birthday party of the century!"

Chapter 23

A day has passed since the events in Washington. It's the afternoon before the opening day of the festival. Hayes, Miller, Umbra Team One, and I have rented a three-bedroom apartment that we're using for a base of operations. Spread out in the apartment is a slew of military-style gear that Umbra Team brought with them. We've set the living room up to be a command center. Three laptops are active, with someone working on them at all times. We hook another laptop up to a projector that displays important information on one wall of the living room. Pinned to one of the other walls is a more detailed map of the large tropical island getaway, courtesy of recent drone footage. We have different areas marked off on the map. There is a camping area with fancy dome-shaped tents that look big enough for two to three people. There are several makeshift restaurants. Also displayed on the map are several beach houses. The beach houses range from modest-looking to some in which a rich celebrity might stay. At the center of the island is a large stage for musical performances.

I walk over to Hayes, who's working on one laptop. "Can I ask you something?"

Not looking up from what she's working on, she replies, "Go ahead, Jeffery."

"How do you guys pay for all of this?"

Hayes stops working on the laptop and looks at me. "How do you think? The government delegates large sums of money so we can complete our tasks. We also gain funds through other means, but that's classified."

"Do other countries have groups similar to AIA?" I ask her.

"Some, yes, but we rarely work with them. They have their way of doing things, and we have ours. There are also organizations that work with the anomalies we monitor."

Before I can ask anything more, Miller begins his briefing. "Okay, everyone, listen up." He's sitting at the laptop that's connected to the projector. Everyone stops what they're doing to turn their attention to him.

Miller taps a button on the laptop, and displayed on the wall are a side-by-side images of Devin and Tiffany. "Our targets are Tiffany Natts and Devin Highmore," he announces. "We believe Tiffany is about to birth to a Summa class anomaly. This is coming down from the Board of Directors. They want her and the anomaly kept alive for study, got it? But if we can't bring them back alive, then we have orders to terminate them."

"I have a question," I say boldly. Miller nods at me. "If whatever is inside Tiffany is basically a god, then why do they want it alive?" I asked.

"AIA researchers study anomalies so we can better combat other anomalies. If whatever inside her is in fact a god-level entity, then it's a gold mine for their research."

"What about Highmore himself? Do they want him alive?" one of the Umbra team members asks.

"The Board says he leaves with us, either walking or in a body bag," Miller answers. He presses the button on the laptop, and projects a birds-eye view of a luxury-style beach house. "Drone footage has led us to believe that this beach house is where both

Highmore and Natts are. We don't have a positive ID, but it's the only beach house with guards outside it round the clock.

"On the first night of the festival," he continues, "there's a concert scheduled. We will split up into two teams, and will set foot on the island at different times. The first team consists of myself, Hayes, and two other agents who will help us out. Our objective is to seek out the suicide bombers. We'll be on the island the moment it's open to the public.

"Team Two will be the Umbra team. You'll come onto the island under cover of darkness and will head directly to the guarded beach house. Chances are, Tiffany at least will be there. She's too pregnant to move around easily. Once you have her, get her off the island." Miller then projects a birds-eye view of a more modest-looking beach house. "This is our base of operations. If anything goes wrong, we'll meet up here."

"Where will I be?" I asked.

"The beach house, mostly, and vlogging. The Board of Directors sees you as a vital part of all of this, Mr. Bailey. The cult hasn't killed you yet, and there must be a reason. Plus, you're still bait."

One member of the Umbra team rolls his eyes at what Miller said. "I find it suspect that you're even here, and even more that you're still alive," he remarks to me.

I look at him, eyes narrowed. "What's that supposed to mean, Beckett?"

"I've read all the files. Stuff isn't adding up here. Highmore wants all this done below the radar, so as not to garner any unwanted attention so that this cult's god can be born. You're here with us, alive and well, and we're heading to an island full of cult members."

Pissed, I get up from my seat and storm over to Beckett. He rises to meet me, and we stand in the center of the living room, staring daggers at one another. His muscular figure towers over my five-five average-built body. He smirks at me. "What are you gonna do, Vlog Boy? Make a video exposing me?" Beckett taunts.

When he says that, I lose it. Everything that's happened to me involving this fucking cult boils to the surface. I ball my hand into a fist, and with all my rage I punch him in the face. He staggers back and runs his fingers across his lips, looking at the bit of blood on them, then at me with eyes full of hate. I know he's about to beat my ass, but at least I got one decent hit in. "You little shit!" Beckett snarls, and lunges at me, taking me to the ground. We scrap around for a few seconds before everyone else in the room dogpiles on top of us and begins prying us apart.

"You have to be deaf, dumb, and blind not to realize that this is a setup!" Beckett yells at Miller.

"Fuck you! I've been trying to get rid of this cult since Day One, like everyone else in this room! One of my friends is dead because of the cult! I have another friend who got brainwashed into joining!" I yell back at him.

"Both of you shut up! Once all this is done, you two can beat each other to a bloody mess for all I care! Until then, both of you calm the fuck down so we can get this done!" Miller looks at me. "You good?"

Beckett and I still stare daggers at each other. I take my gaze off Beckett and look at Miller, nodding, not saying anything. Miller then looks at Beckett. "What about you?"

Beckett side-eyes Miller and nods sharply. "Yeah, I'm good."

Miller nods in approval. "Good. Now, everyone back to work. Anders, come see me about that escape plan."

Chapter 24

It's the afternoon of the opening day of the festival. To say I'm on edge is an understatement. We had to catch a ferryboat to the island. Miller, Hayes, and I spread out on the boat to make it appear that we weren't together, in case the cult is watching me. The other agents that Miller mentioned had taken the ferry this morning to get everything set up. During the ferry ride, I met a few people who follow my vlogs. I made small talk with them and took selfies with them. They asked me what I was doing heading to the festival, and I explained to them that I was just here to see what it was all about.

It takes an hour for the ferry to arrive on the island. When people get off the boat, staff members who are most likely cult members direct us to a check-in station. The closer I get to the front of the line, the more nervous I become. My heart is beating a mile a minute. I'm using my real name to attract attention from the cult, while the agents use fake identities. When I make it to the front of the line, on the surface I'm calm, cool, and collected; but on the inside, I'm an anxious wreck. I hand the staff member my ID, which he takes, and starts to type on his laptop. Then he stops typing, and stares at me for a long moment. I smile. He looks back at the laptop, and then at me again before he hands my ID back, and tells me where I will stay and to enjoy myself. I smile, thanking him, and head towards the beach house I'll stay in, the one Miller told us about.

As I walk away, I look over my shoulder to see where Miller and Hayes are in line, and note that the staff member who checked me in is talking to another staff member, pointing me out. When I notice that, I grow even more nervous and start rushing toward the beach house. While I hurry over, I take out my cellphone and start texting Hayes and Miller.

They know I'm here now. I'm sure they have something planned for me.

And that's a problem because of why again? Miller replies. Bastard.

Hayes' reply is more measured and useful. *Just stay calm. Walk around and start vlogging. Miller will meet up with the rest of the agents. I will monitor you from a distance in case something happens.*

Easier said than done, I reply.

Just do your job so we can do ours, was Miller's response. "Asshole," I mutter.

I head to the beach, looking around to see if anyone is following me. The only person following me is Hayes, and that from a significant distance. When I see her, I breathe a giant sigh of relief.

Once at the beach, I take out my phone and turn the camera on in selfie mode. I hold it up so it faces me and press *Record.* "What's up, guys? Jeffery B. here. I know it's been a long time. Things have gotten more insane with this cult." I pause, trying to figure out what to say next. "This goes beyond the cult, though. It's hard to explain, but I've been told this is a matter of national security, and..." Mid-sentence, I pause, seeing something in the distance. I take the camera out of selfie mode and point it at what I'm seeing. Using the camera like binoculars, I zoom in. I see three individuals looking over and pointing at me. My brain is telling me to haul ass out of there, but it feels as if my shoes are cement blocks. Out of nowhere, a loud, booming, hornlike sound echoes across the island. Panning the camera around and to the sky, I search to see what it is. I put the camera back on the figures as they walk away.

"They're leaving to prep for his arrival," a female voice says behind me. Startled, I turn around to see a woman in her mid-20s with stringy blond hair. He has on a flower print bikini top and a pair of jean shorts. She continues, "That sound you just heard was him gradually breaking through into our world. It's just a matter of time, Jeffery."

"Who are you?" I asked her.

"A follower of The Great Void. Soon, we'll all have the honor of seeing him in this world." She smiles sweetly, then turns and walks away.

"Hey, wait a second, I have more questions!" I reach out, grabbing her wrist, trying to stop her. A soon as I grab her, she reaches into her pocket, taking out a butterfly knife. In a flash, she exposes the blade and slashes me across the forearm. I release her, grabbing onto my own forearm to stop the bleeding. Once released, she rushes away from me, heading toward where I saw the three individuals that pointed me out.

Hayes hurries over to me and examines my wound. She tells me to hurry to the beach house where the other agents are while she chases after the woman who attacked me. Holding my forearm, blood trickling through my fingers, I dash back to the beach house. Once there, I pound on the door frantically. Miller answers the door, and I push my way through. After locking the door, Miller glares at me as I take a seat on the kitchen table. "What happened to you? Where's Hayes?"

"A cultist attacked me. She said that loud noise, that horn sound, was Rojachar trying to enter our world. After the cultist attacked me, she ran away and Hayes went after her."

"Hey, Norm, can you come in here? Bring your medical kit," Miller calls.

A man in swim trunks, flip-flops, and a tacky-looking short-sleeved flower-print shirt comes in with a medical bag. "I'm Norm," he introduces himself.

"Jeffery."

Norm sits his medical bag down on the table and pulls up a chair. "I know, I read the files. Let's look at your arm." I remove my hand so that Norm can look at the wound. "Ah, this isn't too bad. Any deeper and it could have done major damage, though." He reaches into his medical bag, pulling out some things, and works on my forearm.

"You sure?" I asked.

"Yeah, you're good. I was a field medic in the Army. This is refreshing compared to bullet and IED wounds," he told me.

"Thank you for your service," I say automatically.

"You're welcome. I was happy to do it."

I turn my attention back to Miller. "I thought you said two agents would help us?"

"Davidson is out doing recon, looking for anything of interest that might help us," Miller answers.

Hayes enters into the beach house and closes the door behind her, locking it. "Any luck finding her?" I ask.

Hayes shakes her head "No, she must have blended in with the crowd or gone to Devin's place. When I was looking for her, I met up with Davidson. I gave him the description of the woman who attacked you. How's the arm?"

"He'll be fine. It wasn't too bad," Norm says, finishing up.

"Good, we'll need everyone at 100%. Highmore is giving an opening speech tonight to get the festival started. Like an opening ceremony kind of thing. It starts at 8 PM sharp. So rest up, because it'll be a long night," Miller asks.

Later that evening, we all attend the concert. We spread out in the crowd to cover more ground, equipped with milspec earpieces to communicate with one another. While we walk through the crowd, Umbra Team contacts us, letting us know they've arrived and that they're heading straight to Devin Highmore's beach house. I continue looking around for anything that sticks out. It's about all I'm good for at this point. I pause my search when Highmore takes the stage. Once the crowd lays eyes on the bastard, they start cheering in excitement, ready to get the night started.

He grabs the mic from the stand like a rock star, and looks out at the sea of people in a prideful stance, a cocky grin on his face. He wears emerald-green swim trunks, a black short-sleeved shirt, and a pair of flip-flops. "How you doing tonight!?" he hollers. Everyone yells back in excitement. "I'm so glad every one of you could be here for this event. This is a landmark occasion. This is when a golden age of peace is born — a new renaissance in which we will all become one collective mind, doing what we *must* do to make this world a better place. We have individuals from all walks of life here. This is just the beginning, folks. You will all be held in high regard and revered for what you accomplish here." The crowd cheers even more as Devin stands gazing on at them. "Now: let the festivities begin. To open things up, I'd like to introduce to you our newest signing: The very talented singer, Menace Matrix!"

After the introduction, a man in his mid-20s walks on stage. He and Highmore exchange handshakes before Highmore leaves. Everyone cheers in excitement and sings and dances with the ensuing music. Me, I go back to my search. It's like looking for a needle in a needle-stack, but midway through the performance, I spot the girl who attacked me; this time she's wearing a black backpack. We lock eyes. She smiles, takes out her cell phone, and starts messing around it. I press down on my earpiece so everyone can hear me. "Guys, I found the girl that attacked me. I'm gonna..."

Before I can finish my sentence, a bright flash and an incoherent roar of sound emanate from the girl. The explosion rips through the crowd between us, throwing me to the ground hard and crashing me into unconsciousness.

Chapter 25

When I come to, a deafening ringing is all I can hear at first. My vision is blurred. It takes a few minutes for my hearing and vision to return to normal, and what I see is total carnage. I hear people crying out in pain, and the ground is littered with people who are dead or on death's doorstep. People who can are tending to their friends, yelling for help. I reach my hand up to my earpiece to get hold of the agents, but my earpiece isn't there anymore. Most likely it fell out during the blast.

I take out my phone and try calling Miller and Hayes. Neither answers; the calls go straight to voicemail. I leave messages saying that I'm okay and to call me back ASAP. After my fuzziness clears a bit more, I remember them saying that if anything went wrong; we were to head to the beach house. Before I leave for the beach house, though, I look at the destruction caused by the cult. Everyone needs to know the truth before it gets covered up, I decide.

I put my camera in selfie mode and pressed *Record*. "Jeffrey Bailey here," I begin in a ragged voice. I realize I'm breathing hard, too. "I'm still here on Cleo Marie Island. Its 8:21 PM, Friday, May 17th, 2021. I'm at the music festival Highmore Entertainment organized. Everything was fine until a massive explosion went off here during the Menace Matrix concert, killing or and harming everyone here, including me. There was a girl with a backpack, and my guess is she had a bomb in her bag. She was messing with her phone just before it blew. I'm guessing she was some kind of suicide bomber.

"I've also learned that The Order of the Void is trying to bring the so-called god they worship into this world. In order for that to happen, a mass sacrifice has to occur. What better way to get a lot of sacrifices together in one spot than to offer a concert by a hot new artist?" I switch the camera out of selfie mode so I can film the aftermath of the damage caused by the explosion.

After five minutes or so of grisly footage that almost makes me puke, I switch the camera back to selfie mode. "The government is involved in fighting this cult, and has been for a long time. There's this government agency called the Abnormal Investigation Agency. They specialize in handling paranormal cases, occult issues, and other stuff that normal law enforcement can't handle. Two AIA agents contacted me because they noticed my vlogs about the cult. Long story short, we've been working together.

"We found out that Tiffany Natts, a girl who has been missing for over a year, is a member of the cult and is meant to give birth to their god so he can be here on Earth. The investigation led us here. I have no idea if the agents I'm working with are still alive or not. Devin Highmore has a beach house here, though, and I'm heading there now. I'm getting answers and stopping this before anyone else has to die." I switch the camera off and upload the video to my vlog, and also send it to Natalie, in case something happens to me.

When I finish, I get a call from Miller, thank God.

"Are you and Hayes okay?" I ask in a panicked voice as I start jogging toward the beach house.

"We're fine. Where are you now?"

"I'm heading to Devin's beach house. I'm getting answers and ending this tonight," I declare.

"Negative! Bailey. just head to *our* beach house. The other agents and I will handle this." Miller pauses. "Umbra Team is heading to Highmore's place now. Let the professionals handle this. Just head back to the beach house."

I lose it. "*Professionals*!? If it weren't for me, the AIA wouldn't have gotten this far!"

"Jeffery, this is Agent Hayes. You're on speakerphone. Let us handle this, please. Things will get dangerous for you if you go."

Fuck that.

I hang up and rush over to Devin Highmore's house; it takes me a good 15 minutes to get there. When I arrive, I slide behind a tree to look for any guards or anything that stands out; oddly, nothing does. Is he that confident he can't be stopped? Feeling uneasy, I use the camera on my phone as binoculars to zoom in on the house to see if I could see inside any of the windows; but the black curtains are closed, so I can't. I'll have to get closer, maybe even storm the place myself. Nervously, I creep up to the house, making my way to the back, trying to find a way inside. When I turn

the corner, I bump into a man wearing an emerald-green cloak. My

eyes go wide with panic and fear; I immediately turn around, only to

bump into another cloaked person, and trip and fall on my ass.

Before I can get up, I hear a gun being cocked. "Get up, slowly," one

of the cloaked ones orders me. I obey.

"Where are we going?" I ask them.

"Walk," orders the same man, his gun's muzzle pressed into

the middle of my back. The full moon lights our path forward. We

proceed along a densely wooded path; the deeper into the woods we

get, the more the cries of pain and horror from the beach fade, and

the more the glowing light of a fire becomes clear. Ahead, I can also

hear people chanting, "Praise The Great Void, praise The Great

Devourer, praise Rojachar." While they chant, I can hear woman

groaning and yelling.

We leave the wooded path and enter a large open area.

Spaced around the clearing are many tiki torches, illuminating

dozens of green-cloaked figures with their arms and hands in the air,

chanting loudly. In the center of all this is Tiffany Natts, lying on a birthing table with her feet placed on stirrups. A doctor and a nurse are telling Tiffany to *push*. Highmore stands next to her, doing the same.

Tiffany screams in pain one more time. As she yells, the fire from the torches fades from its original color and burns pure emerald green; and the child is born.

A deep, reverberating chord echoes over the island again.

Looking pleased with himself, as if he's the one who did all the work, the doctor cuts the umbilical cord and walks over to a portable cleaning station next to Tiffany that's equipped with everything needed to spruce up the baby. Meanwhile, Devin looks at Tiffany, smiling proudly. "You did great!" he proclaims. "We're all proud of you, but HE is especially grateful to you." Devin turns away from her and looks at me. He raises his hand, signaling for the chanting to stop. The cloaked ones quiet down as the fire returns to normal. "Ah, Jeffery! There you are. Come forward; I've been waiting for you, my man."

The cult member with the gun pushes me forward. I walk towards Devin, stopping just a few feet in front of him. "What *is* all this?" I ask, though I've pretty much got it all figured out.

Devin smiles widely, from ear to ear. "It's the birth of The Great Void. Rojachar is here on Earth now." As Devin speaks, the doctor hands the baby to Tiffany. She smiles and begins to breastfeed the child. "Everything is now in place," Devin continues. He motions to Tiffany and the child. "The Great Void and the Mother of the Void are here." He suddenly points to me. "And now the Voice of the Void is here as well."

I look at him, confused and panicky. "The fuck are you talking about?" I demand.

Devin Highmore says smoothly, "The Voice of the Void is just what it sounds like, buddy: a voice to spread the holy word of Rojachar. To educate the masses. To be a leader, and usher in a new world — a world where our Lord Rojachar and everyone in it is of one mind. Soon the world will be at peace at last, the only peace that can possibly exist without eliminating every single human on the planet! The man who held my position in the organization before me went on and on, saying *he* was the Voice of the Void. He wasn't; no, he was a false prophet. So I did what was necessary for the betterment of the world. I killed him and took his place."

Devin paces back and forth. "Then I started thinking: am *I* the Voice of the Void? Am *I* the one meant to lead the world to Rojachar?" Devin shook his head. "I concluded that I was not. My role was to *find* the Voice of the Void. Then He spoke to me." Devin looks over his shoulder, smiling at the baby, and then back to me. "And you came along. You educated the masses about us and Rojachar. *You* were His voice."

I shake my head. "You're fucking crazy. This whole cult is crazy! You want to take everyone's free will away! You killed my friend!"

"Jeffery, Jeffery, we did no such a thing. We were going to, admittedly, but someone beat us to it," Devin explains.

I look at him, confused. "What? I don't get it. He made a video saying you guys were after him. A source told me that the Order killed him. I mean, if you didn't want people to know about the cult, why the video on the deep web? Why come into my livestream and talk about the cult?"

Devin walks over to me, slowly, hands in the pockets of his green cloak. "I needed to bring the cult into the Digital Age to find you, Jeffery. The Voice of the Void. It was risky, I admit, but He guided me down the right path to find you. That's the reason we posted that video. That's the reason we came into your livestream to help spread the word."

"And Bret? What about him?" I asked.

Devin shakes his head. "We didn't kill him. As you know, we have people from all walks of life who praise The Great Void, from people who bag groceries at the local supermarket to powerful national-level politicians. Even people inside the AIA. That's right, we know about them. We have eyes and ears there. My sources said they would use Bret as bait. At the time, we believed your friend was The Voice of the Void. We were going to talk to him, Jeffery, not kill him. Before I had people even leave my HQ to confront your friend, my sources in the AIA said that agents had already killed him, because he wouldn't go along with what they wanted him to do. So they found you instead — and so did we, through His guidance."

I stood there, not knowing what to say. I finally croaked, "No, that's not true. It can't be true. You killed Bret."

"I assure you, Jeffery, we did not. We want to usher in an age of peace. One collective mind. A world that future generations can be proud of."

"Peace?!" I shout. "You're talking about eliminating free will! About everyone having the same thought process!"

"And what has free will done for us?" Devin asks in a reasonable tone. "Even in America, the most democratic of countries, it has given us a flawed justice system where the rich get away with everything, while ordinary people who commit petty crimes have the entire weight of the justice system thrown at them. Government officials use their status to achieve their own selfish goals to better their own lives, not the lives of the people that elected them. CEOs give themselves million-dollar bonuses, while their workers live paycheck to paycheck. People use religion to justify murder. It was free will that killed Bret."

"What makes you different from them? You've killed in the name of your god! You just killed dozens, if not hundreds, of innocent people with the bomb at your concert, a bomb set off by one of your cult members!"

"But that's what separates me from the people using you for their own goals," Devin says, spreading his arms wide. "I sacrificed people in pursuit of a better, more just world where everyone has everything they need, and everyone is happy, because all are one. The souls of my sacrifices gave The Great Void energy to come to this plane." He smiles disarmingly.

"You kill so you can take away people's freedom!" I yell.

"True, Jeffery, but I kill to make the world a better place." Still smiling, he looks over at the cult member behind me. "Give him your gun, Peter," Devin says to him.

"Mr. Highmore?" the cult member questions.

"Give him your gun. Trust me," Devin says reassuringly.

Peter steps from behind me and in front of me, handing me the gun, and steps aside. Devin steps forward into my personal space. Taking the hand that holds the gun in his own, the cult leader places the muzzle of the gun on his forehead. "No matter what happens, no one does anything!" Devin yells to the rest of his people. Then he turns his attention back to me.

"You speak of free will, and how it would be a terrible thing if it were gone. Here is your chance to save it and everyone else. Kill me. Kill Rojachar and Tiffany. It's still possible. You still think we killed your friend? Now is the time to get your revenge. Become the hero of a broken world that's beyond repair. Or put the gun down and become what you're meant to be: The Voice of the Void. The leader of a world full of nothing but peace. A world filled with eight billion happy people who have everything they need, forever."

I stand there holding the gun, still pointed at his forehead, thinking about everything he's said. Maybe he's lying; maybe he's telling the truth. And would it be so bad for the world to be eternally peaceful, assuming he *is* telling the truth? He certainly seems to believe it. I consider everything I've gone through, everything I've discovered. I think about what Natalie said about her little brother dying in prison thanks to a corrupt judge. The corrupt become more corrupt. The greedy become greedier. Everyone else suffers. I think about Bret. Maybe it *was* the AIA that killed my friend and tempted me into this odyssey of pain. Maybe Devin's right. I lower the gun slowly.

"Good, Jeffery, put the gun down. Help me, help *us* make this world a better place," Devin says soothingly.

"Everyone freeze! Party's over!" Miller yells, coming out the shadows of the woods along with Hayes and the Umbra team. The cult members and Devin look unfazed upon seeing the Umbra team armed with their automatic weapons, all of which are aimed at Devin, Tiffany, and her godling.

"Stay calm, everyone!" Devin calls, holding his hands up in the air as if to declare victory. He walks over to Miller with a large smile on his face. "I don't know who are, but I know you and your friends are from the AIA. You're too late. The Voice, the Mother, and the God are all here. You've lost."

Miller laughs and raises an eyebrow as if to say, *You've gotta be kidding me.* "You know we have guns and you don't, right? You have two opinions, Highmore: come with us alive or in a body bag.

Our job is to get the girl and the kid. Taking you alive just gets us a bonus on our paychecks."

Everyone stands there in silence. I look at both Miller and Devin, wondering what will happen next. All that can be heard in that moment is the freshening wind blowing through the trees, and the crackling of the torches, which have become tinged with green again.

"Fire," Miller says calmly.

With that said, gunfire rings out. For me, instinct takes over. I drop the gun in my hand so, hopefully, the agents won't kill me when they see it, and rush to Tiffany and the baby through the hail of gunfire. Miraculously, not a single bullet hits me. I huddle over the two of them, using my body as a shield. Over the sound of gunfire, I can hear both Tiffany and the baby screaming in terror.

What seems like hours really only takes seconds. When the gunfire stops, I open my eyes and pat myself down to see if they shot me. To my surprise, I'm still not hit, though I find several bullet holes in my bright green hoodie. Thank God my phone is intact. I wonder if little Rojachar protected me somehow. Tiffany whimpers, curled in a fetal position, holding her crying baby tight. I check them; they're both unharmed as well.

Devin and the rest of the cult members, however, are not: they lie bloodied and dead on the ground. In a fit of rage, I rush over and punch Miller as hard as I can in the face. It barely fazes him. "You bastard! You could have killed us!" I scream.

As one man, the Umbra team turn their guns toward me. With his head turned to the side because of the punch, Miller spits out a little blood and orders, "Lower your weapons." The Umbra team obeys. "You're right," he admits, "but I didn't. Thanks to you, a mighty blow has been dealt to the Rojachar cult. Word will get around to the rest of the assholes that Highmore is dead. That'll leave a vacuum of power, and the top ranks will start fighting for power and leadership. The cult will rip itself apart from the inside out. Then AIA teams will come in and take care of any remnants of the cult."

Miller holds out his right hand, and I just stare at it. My own hands are jammed in the front pockets of my hoodie, and I don't take them out. "Jeffery Bailey," Miller announces, "you should be proud of yourself. You will be an unsung national and global hero. Gone and forgotten by most, but on behalf of the AIA, I would like to thank you for everything you've done."

I make no move to shake his hand.

Shrugging, Miller lowers his hand and turns to Anders. "Have half your team take the girl and the kid to the extraction point, while the other half raids the beach house. Grab anything of interest. Computers, important documents, everything."

Anders nods and shouts, "You heard the suit, team! The sooner we do this, sooner we can go home!" Half the men head inside while the others head over to Tiffany and baby, and usher them away from the area.

I stand there, still confused as hell at everything going on. I watch as they take the girl and the baby away. "What's going on?" I finally ask, my voice weak.

"Classified," Hayes answers.

"What happens now? Why were you speaking in the past tense about me?" I ask them. I start to bring my hands out of my hoodie's pocket, but stop when Miller's hand goes to his gun.

"I know you still have your gun," he growls. "That's far enough." And it is, actually.

Hayes takes out her cell phone. She holds it up, and on screen is the video I made in the aftermath of the explosion. "Our tech guys caught it in time, before it could be uploaded to the web and emailed to your friend." Hayes sighs heavily. "I'm sorry, Jeffery, I really am, but this is where we part ways. Permanently."

Miller pulls out his gun and points it at my head. "If only you hadn't tried to upload that video. It's okay, though: if it makes you feel any better, this would have been the outcome anyway. You're a loose end, just like your friend Bret was. The AIA can't afford to have the public knowing that it exists. Besides, kid, you were just bait. Useful bait, but bait nonetheless. It's nothing personal. And don't worry — your family will be well compensated for your dying in the line of duty. Look at it as the AIA saying 'Thank you' for a job well done. Your folks, like the rest of the public, will be told that this was just an act of domestic terrorism performed by a crazed concert-goer.

"Thank you once again for all your help," Miller says, not one iota of remorse in his voice. At least Hayes' eyes are tearing up, even if she doesn't stop him.

I look down the barrel of the gun, thinking, *So this is it.* Everything I did was all for nothing. None of this will make it out to the public. The world will continue spinning, not knowing what has happened here. My body filled with rage, I lift both hands out of my hoodie's pockets, middle fingers extended in one last great act of defiance, and scream, *"Fuck you!"*

The last thing I hear is the bang of the gun, as something smashes into my forehead. I see a flash, and reach for it.

Then darkness.

Chapter 26

Five months have passed since the fiasco on Cleo Marie Island. Agent Cleve Miller stands in front of a prison cell tucked into the rear of a large, crowded laboratory filled with busy scientists. The wall facing the laboratory is made out of thick plexiglass. Miller knocks on it. "Good afternoon, Tiffany. How are you today?"

The sound of a flushing toilet can be heard from behind a privacy wall in the cell. A haggard-looking Tiffany Natts shuffles out from behind the wall and walks up to the plexiglass. "Where is my baby?" she asks for the thousandth time.

Miller smirks a bit at the question, and as usual, refuses to answer. "How was lunch? I heard you had baked chicken breasts and a salad."

"I want my baby," she demands.

"I had a meatball sub. I know, I know. I should have gone with a salad, but it's been a long day, and a good lunch can make a long day better. Hayes was going to come, but she's still busy with the Cleo Marie clean-up."

Tiffany yells and bangs on the glass, demanding her child back. During her outburst, Miller takes out his phone and holds it up to the glass so she can see. Her rage soon turns into sobbing. On the phone is a picture of her child playing with some blocks. She runs her fingers against the glass, as if she's touching the child in person. "I took it this morning," Miller tells her. "Subject 171 is fine. In fact, he's healthier and maturing much faster than most babies."

Tiffany continues sobbing. "Please, I just want to hold him for a few seconds!"

Miller puts the phone away. "You can't. That could be *very* dangerous. I just wanted to show you that Baby Ro is alive and well. You two are very special to the AIA, you see. Maybe in time, you'll see each other again — but we have many more tests to run on both of you. If you're lucky and keep doing as you're told, maybe I'll give you a video of him soon. Now, if you'll excuse me, I have other matters to tend to." Miller turns his back to her as she falls to the floor, crying out for her baby.

Miller walks over to the lead scientist. "Dr. Toddmore. How are things coming?"

A bald man in his mid-40s turns away from what he's working on. "Ah, Agent Miller. Let me start off by saying that this project is truly fascinating, combining elements of the occult and modern science to produce something no less than a match made in heaven. Thank you for bringing me in on it." His smile fades to a thoughtful expression. "There *is* a slight hiccup."

"Hiccup? Doctor you have a blank check from the AIA. The word 'hiccup' should be nonexistent in your vocabulary regarding this project."

"Agent Miller, we can get all the data and run all the tests on the mother that we like. It's just, with the child..."

"What about the child, Dr. Toddmore?"

"That's just it, Agent Miller. Subject 171 is just five months old, and we are very limited on what it can and cannot do—"

Miller grabs the doctor by the lapels of his lab coat and yanks him off the ground, pinning him to the wall. "Doctor, the Board of Directors has tasked me with seeing this project to the end.

I don't care if you have to tear that that child apart and stitch him back together. If you can't handle this project, then I will find someone who can. Patience is not my strongest virtue. I want a prototype of the God Gene ready to go ASAP. Do I make myself clear?" Miller demands in a cold, harsh tone.

The doctor nods, fearful, not wanting to know what will happen if he refuses. "Yes, sir, I understand."

Epilog

In a bunker five hundred feet below Miller and Toddmore, we play with our blocks, and I come to a conclusion. I now understand what to do and how to do it. Rojachar, whose pudgy little body I share, approves. I, the Voice of the Void, open our mouth and say in an ancient language that my handlers will surely mistake as baby talk, "Let there be dark."

And there *is* dark, and we see that it is good. In the milliseconds before the backup generators kick in, I nudge loose two files in the AIA's primary server: my video of the aftermath of the explosion at the Cleo Marie Island concert, and the video of my execution by Miller, which I filmed surreptitiously in the last moments of my life through a bullet hole in my hoodie. When the lights come back on, both files are uploaded into the Cloud, my worried followers — including Natalie — receive an email to that effect, and a thousand hackers are alerted of a backdoor into the AIA's servers.

Baby Ro grins widely and smacks his lips. To their eternal regret, his handlers mistake his behavior for gas pains.

THE END

CPSIA information can be obtained
at www.ICGtesting.com
Printed in the USA
LVHW111623031120
670604LV00006B/81